# APE MAN

*Doc Beck Westerns Book 8*

## SARAH ELISABETH SAWYER

RockHaven Publishing
P.O. Box 1103
Canton, Texas 75103



Editor: Lynda Kay Sawyer
Cover Design: Mollie E. Reeder
Author Photo by R. A. Whiteside. Courtesy of the National Museum of the American Indian, Smithsonian Institution
Print ISBN: 978-1-956043-05-1

# PROLOGUE

There was just the right amount of light in the dark interior of the ringmaster's wagon as Calvin Blackthorn poured another shot of whiskey for his drinking companion. Will Flit was the sideshow manager, and Calvin wanted him nice and drunk before he killed him.

Flit accepted the shot glass and raised it in a toast at Calvin. "To the next town."

With the usual salute, Flit downed the drink and smacked his lips. He was still dressed in his gray suit and orange vest, though he'd ripped his tie loose right after the show ended. A slender and careless man, he would present no challenge.

There was a long night ahead, but Calvin had waited two years to exact this revenge, and there was no need to hurry now. Everything would be set in motion this night, though it would be far from over for days yet.

Calvin Blackthorn was a patient man. Very patient. And few men could match his imposing six-foot four height that drew ladies of the circus to watch him lift the strongman's weights each morning.

Will Flit clunked his glass on the table, then wagged his finger at Calvin. "You've been with us what, three weeks now? I've never seen audiences so taken with the man in the stovepipe hat. You're good for the Donovan Brothers Circus."

Calvin tipped the whiskey bottle to fill his own glass and Flit's again. He spoke softly. "And don't forget the sideshow. You're the best manager for our most popular exhibit."

Flit snorted, bringing the glass to his puffy lips. "That part's not so hard. It's only half man, half ape."

He chuckled into his glass before taking a sip, then downed the whole shot.

Calvin smiled congenially. *Just keep drinking and talking, Flit. You're making this easy.*

Calvin brought his drink to his mouth to pretend he was drinking equally. But one shot was enough for him, unlike some men who needed several to bolster their courage for what he was about to do.

It was past 1AM, but most of the circus camp was just settling down for the night. They'd spent the last two hours packing for the move to the next town. They only stayed in most places for one performance. Small Wyoming towns weren't unlike all the other towns before and the ones ahead, with pockets barely deep enough to support a struggling circus.

Calvin's fake résumé fit in well with the hodgepodge of strange souls and shady characters that made up the Donovan Brothers Circus. He'd never been part of a circus, but who checked references? Certainly not the circus manager, Allen Jones, who was desperate for a ringmaster after his disappeared three weeks ago. Calvin was even able to influence Jones to add an upcoming stop for the circus—Centennial Ridge.

Calvin appreciated how things happened so conveniently. Of course, they would. He was the one who made them happen.

Flit was even more foolish than the circus manager. He had a big mouth, too. Calvin hadn't liked him from the moment they met and hearing him talk about the ape man tonight left him with no regret in his plan to take Will Flit's life.

The man set his tumbler on the table and stretched his arms wide in the tight space of the wood-encased wagon that had become Calvin's home when he joined the circus. Part kitchen, part bedroom, part parlor. All hate.

Flit rubbed his eyes. "Reckon I'll turn in, be a big show tomorrow in Cheyenne. The two-day stays are better than one. Gives a fellow time to meet the local ladies."

Calvin stayed slouched in his chair, holding his shot glass by the rim. "You ought to take the ape man with you. He draws attention everywhere he goes."

Flit snorted. "That's not what I had in mind. Wouldn't take that half-man anywhere. His days of living life and enjoying the company of ladies are long gone."

Calvin slowly nodded, lowering his glass to the table and setting it down silently.

Yes, the ape man's days of living life were long over. So were Will Flit's, a fact the drunk man didn't yet know.

Flit planted his hands on his knees and pushed to his feet, partly doubled over, groaning from fatigue and strain on his body that spent too many years traveling dusty roads. Those days were over.

He stretched wide again, fingertips nearly touching the sides of the narrow ringmaster wagon. He puffed out a smelly breath and lifted his glass in final salute.

"To the Donovan Brothers Circus, a poorly named caravan that doesn't contain any brothers."

Calvin Blackthorn rose and clicked glasses with his victim.

"So they say."

He let Flit down his shot glass, then Calvin tipped his head in another salute. "Like you said, to the next town. Cheyenne."

And the town after that, and the town after that. Then, to the final leg of Calvin's vengeance quest: Centennial Ridge, Wyoming, and the famed Doc Beck.

# CHAPTER 1

The mahogany grandfather clock struck, its clang echoing down the gilded hallways of the Wyoming state capitol building. The metallic sound of the pendulum nearly sent Doctor Rebekah LaRoche out of her skin.

Instead, she calmed herself by twisting her reticule straps tight around her gloved hands, cutting off the circulation in her fingers.

The clock struck again, a total of ten times. After the echo died away, she relaxed and her fingers started tingling.

Just Jimmy, seated in the chair next to her outside Senator Jeffrey Harris' office, leaned toward her. "You all right, Miss Rebekah?"

Jimmy hadn't spoken above a whisper since they entered the capitol building in Cheyenne. The rotunda alone scared him half to death. It was painted in trompe l'oeil style, to "fool the eye." From the third floor, the checkerboard floors created a three-dimensional illusion in the open center. Rebekah had to hold onto his skinny arm to steady him.

While Rebekah was grateful to give Jimmy the educational

opportunity of visiting the capitol, she could hardly hold herself together with his constant worry. But he was truly trying to help.

She let out a slow breath, releasing the hold on her reticule in favor of tightening a pin in her hat.

"I am a little nervous, Jimmy. Senator Harris promised to meet us early so we could prepare for the governor's arrival."

"Want me to knock again?"

Rebekah shook her head. Her pins couldn't hold her hat any tighter, nor could the state capitol squeeze her heart tighter. There was no one in Senator Harris's office, not even his assistant.

They'd arrived at 9:30AM. After a twenty minute wait her uncle, Doctor Robert T. McKinnon, had finally departed to try and find someone who knew something.

But now it was 10AM, their designated meeting time with the Nebraskan governor. Rebekah and Jimmy still sat alone outside the senator's office. Rebekah only hoped the closed door of the office wasn't foreshadowing a closed door on her return to the Omaha Indian Reservation.

Her recent incident with Cord and Ella Johnson landed in newspapers, and all reported wildly different stories about what ended in a deadly encounter. None of the stories were front page, but not all were favorable, either.

Jimmy, dressed in the only suit he'd ever owned, began talking again, still in a whisper. He was attempting to distract her, but she was afraid of being distracted. She needed her wits and focus like never before.

"Miss Rebekah, I'm sure excited about Pastor Wharton planning my baptism before cold weather sets in. I'm just hoping some of the boys from the ranch will join me. Think they will? Ma'am?"

Rebekah murmured, "Perhaps, Jimmy."

"I'm grateful Doc McKinnon is letting us do it at Omaha Lake. Is it true that you named his biggest lake on the ranch when you were a kid?"

"Yes."

"Say, when were you baptized, Miss Rebekah?"

Rebekah began wrapping the straps of the reticule around her gloved fingers one by one. "I believe I was baptized as a child on the reservation. I cannot recall at the moment."

The memory tried to settle in her mind, but she shooed it away. This wasn't the time for sentiments.

Jimmy intertwined his long fingers in his lap, staring at them. "Must've been tough for you, ma'am, growing up on a reservation. Like being a prisoner or something."

Rebekah forced her eyes away from the hallway and looked at Jimmy. But she wasn't really looking at him. She was seeing beyond him to the verdant meadows and breathtaking sunsets of her homeland.

"On the contrary, Jimmy. I had a good childhood. Surrounded by family and Omaha elders. I went to school in the winter, and out on the prairies in the summers to learn my peoples' lifeways. It was...quite wonderful."

"Then how come you never talk about it?"

The meadows in Rebekah's memory faded, replaced by an ominous thundercloud. "Because it's all gone."

Jimmy quickly stood, shattering the vision fully. She followed his line of sight to see Doctor McKinnon striding toward them, a young man at his side. Rebekah recognized the man as Stanley Cook, Senator Harris's assistant.

At last. Her wait was nearly over.

Yet the intensity on Stanley Cook's face left Rebekah giving her reticule one last twist as she stood. The assistant skipped greetings as he went straight to the door, a key ring jingling.

He muttered, "I don't understand why the senator hasn't come for you. He sent me downstairs in case the governor arrived early. We certainly don't want to miss greeting the governor."

Stanley Cook fumbled the key when he tried to insert it in the lock. He took a quick breath and inserted it again. The sheen of sweat on his brow and his shallow breathing was evidence of high stress. Was the senator such a hard man? That didn't bode well for Rebekah's quest.

The fact that the door was locked made Rebekah wonder if the senator was inside. Perhaps he had gone to a lounge.

The tumblers gave way and Stanley Cook pushed the door open.

Doctor McKinnon followed the assistant inside, Rebekah behind them, hesitant because the room was dark. Stanley Cook turned up the gas lamp to reveal his desk in the reception room.

He crossed the room and rapped soundly on the other door—the senator's office. No sunlight streamed in the reception room. The curtains were drawn on the only window.

Stanley Cook put his hand on the doorknob, hesitated, then rapped on the door again. "Senator Harris? Doctor McKinnon and Doctor LaRoche here to see you."

No response. Stanley Cook opened the unlocked door. That room, too, was dark. He crossed the room, heading toward the senator's desk and the unlit lamp on it.

He'd almost reached the desk when he stumbled, took a step back, then released a strangled cry.

Doctor McKinnon hurried into the dark room, Rebekah close behind him. When he halted, she sidestepped to see what he and Stanley Cook were staring at. Jimmy came to her side and let out a mixed gasp and gulp.

"Gracious, Doc Beck, is he..."

Doctor McKinnon knelt on the floor beside the still form of Senator Jeffrey Harris.

Rebekah slowly lowered down beside her uncle Robert, who gazed at the man he considered a friend.

Senator Harris lay face down, blood soaking the cowhide rug that covered the space in front of his desk. Rebekah reached out steady fingers and pressed them against the senator's neck, though she already knew the answer.

She closed her eyes, swallowed, and lowered her hand. "He's dead."

# CHAPTER 2

For an hour, Rebekah remained still, seated in Stanley Cook's reception room. The hands on the gold-faced wall clock ticked off minutes that no longer mattered.

Senator Jeffrey Harris was dead and no one understood how or why.

In and out came multiple professionals—Cheyenne city doctors, state senators, assistants, and newspaper reporters. The town marshal was there along with two of his deputies to corral the people flowing around what he dubbed "a hideous crime scene."

Jimmy wandered between the senator's office and the reception room until Doctor McKinnon finally asked him to sit with Rebekah.

Jimmy fidgeted and mumbled to her about how sorry he was, and how bad he felt for the senator's family, which was primarily two adult children in college back east.

Rebekah couldn't respond, trying to capture the thoughts pinging in her mind—sorrow for the death of a respected man, and how suddenly her opportunity to return home was lost.

With the word *assassination*, well-meaning acquaintances whisked the governor onto a train back to Nebraska. Rebekah hadn't even seen the man who could help her return to the Omaha Indian Reservation.

She closed her eyes. Jimmy patted her arm. "It'll be all right, Miss Rebekah. The Good Lord can still make a way."

His words caused her to smile as she opened her eyes and squeezed Jimmy's hand in return.

"You always know just the right thing to say, Jimmy."

He blushed. "Well, not always, ma'am. But I know the truth because I've lived it."

The town marshal, George Phillips, appeared from the office, a piece of paper in hand as he glanced around. Behind him came orderlies who carried a stretcher with a blanket-covered body. Senator Jeffrey Harris.

Marshal Phillips pointed at Rebekah with the paper he held.

"Are you Doc Beck?"

Rebekah nodded and rose slowly. Senator Harris likely had a note with her western nickname on his desk. Doctor McKinnon emerged from the office, hands in his pockets and eyes sorrowful.

He intercepted the marshal's next question. "What did you find, George?"

The marshal sighed and handed the paper to Doctor McKinnon, then spoke to Rebekah. "There's a busted window latch in there. Likely how the killer got in and out, though it beats me how he could've done it before Jeffrey—Senator Harris—got his pistol out. But it was this note tucked in his shirt pocket that's really got me stumped."

Doctor McKinnon was frowning as he studied the paper. Rebekah stepped forward, holding her hand out. Doctor McKinnon hesitated then handed the note to her, meeting her eyes with his gray ones, more confused now than grieved.

Rebekah took the paper and scanned the typed note:

*Doc Beck is hazardous to one's health.*

A chill swept Rebekah from head to toe. Her hands began to shake, though whether from anger or grief, she couldn't say. Senator Jeffrey Harris was dead because of her—how could that possibly be?

# CHAPTER 3

The sound of a horse trotting up the gravel road leading to Doctor McKinnon's ranch house caused Rebekah to lift her eyes from the book she was reading. Actually, she wasn't reading, only staring at the pages by the lamplight in the parlor.

Laramie Jones came to his feet, hand resting on the butt of his six-gun as he crossed the room to look out the front window. His actions were calm, precise, but Rebekah still felt her heart jitter.

After Marshal Phillips questioned Doctor McKinnon, Rebekah, and Jimmy about their business with Senator Harris, Doctor McKinnon rushed them to the train depot where they barely caught the westbound out of Cheyenne, back to Centennial Ridge. Both he and Jimmy were alert, watching every move of every passenger in the train car.

Now that Rebekah was safe in the ranch house, Doctor McKinnon was still not taking chances. He assigned Laramie Jones to be Rebekah's guard until the killer was caught. Steve Bowers was now temporary foreman of the ranch, with Lucky Saunders as deputy foreman, and Jimmy head wrangler for now. Jimmy objected, wanting to take his place at Rebekah's other side.

But no harm would come to her as long as Laramie was there. Rebekah knew this, yet still reached for her pepperbox laying on the table by the lamp.

Laramie tipped back the curtain with two fingers to peer out into the yard in front of the house. Some of the hands had staked torches around to keep the house illuminated through the night. Laramie wasn't the only one on guard. Rebekah couldn't be safer inside Fort Knox.

The hoofbeats came closer, reaching the front of the house. Rebekah whispered, "Who is it?"

Laramie let the curtain fall and headed to the foyer, hand still close to his six-gun. But his years of experience as a cavalry officer kept him so calm it made Rebekah nervous.

"It's that newspaperman. Hamilton."

Rebekah relaxed, taking her hand off her pepperbox. Michael Hamilton was flamboyant, but harmless. Laramie met him during her risky escapade with Cord and Ella Johnson, but it didn't look like Laramie planned to offer the reporter a friendly greeting.

He called down the hallway toward Doctor McKinnon's study, "Doc, we got company."

Through the open parlor doors, Rebekah watched as Doctor McKinnon joined Laramie, who was opening the door before Michael Hamilton could knock. She recognized Hamilton's loud voice as Doctor McKinnon allowed him in.

Laramie looked ready to send the reporter packing and Rebekah wouldn't mind if he did. She was exhausted and confused. The last thing she wanted was a newspaperman asking questions she could not answer.

Michael Hamilton strode into the parlor and swept off his derby hat with the hand that held a pencil entwined in his fingers, his tablet in his other hand. His brown mustache, the white in it growing more pronounced each time she saw him, twitched when he spoke.

"Well, good evening, Miss Doc Beck. Just can't stay out of trouble, can you?"

Laramie snatched Hamilton's derby hat like an ill-trained butler, then used the hat to point at the man.

"Senator Jeffrey Harris's murder had nothing to do with Doctor LaRoche."

Michael Hamilton looked between Laramie and Rebekah, then whistled long as he flipped pages on his tablet.

"Not according to what I got here from Marshal Phillips. He found a note that said, and I quote, "Doc Beck is hazardous—"

Doctor McKinnon interrupted quietly, "We know what the note said."

Michael Hamilton stilled. He slowly flipped his notes to a blank page as he looked at Rebekah.

"I know it wasn't your fault, Doctor LaRoche. But there's a killer on the loose and he's got you marked. Any idea why?"

Rebekah shook her head, her neck stiff from the day. She should have drawn a nice hot bath an hour ago then gone to bed.

Michael Hamilton's question left her feeling utterly depleted. It was a question she'd wanted to ask herself all day but couldn't seem to grasp that simple word.

*Why?*

She swayed and Doctor McKinnon took her elbow to guide her back to the chair where she settled and shook her head again.

"I have no idea, Mr. Hamilton."

Even as she said the words, Rebekah wasn't sure they were true. After Michael Hamilton's article about her at the Hope Academy in the old mission in New Mexico, there were a lot of people across the West who now knew who she was and what her life was about, carrying on medical missions.

There was one person who did not want her doing that. But she could not fathom Agent Roger Graham murdering a U.S. senator over it. He harbored a deep and unrelenting grudge against Doctor Rebekah LaRoche, but their battle was between them. He wouldn't kill an innocent man to keep her off the Omaha Indian Reservation.

Would he?

Rebekah must not have done well at hiding her thoughts from her face. Michael Hamilton dragged a footstool close to her chair and plopped on it. He began writing something on his tablet.

Doctor McKinnon sighed. "Mr. Hamilton, we're all exhausted. I know it's a long ride back to Centennial Ridge and you're welcome to stay the night in the bunkhouse, but I'm asking you now to leave my niece to rest."

Michael Hamilton shot back to his feet, his gust cooling Rebekah's warm face.

"You're Rebekah's uncle? How could I not have known that?"

His pencil went to his tablet again but the tip never touched paper.

Laramie pinched the pencil between two fingers and slid it out of Hamilton's hand. He plopped the derby hat on the man's head, then snapped the pencil in two.

"Steve will show you to the bunkhouse if you've got a mind to spend the night," Laramie drawled. "He's watching from outside along with a dozen of our men, waiting to shoot anyone who bothers Miss Rebekah."

Michael Hamilton, his derby hat perched comically to one side of his head, grinned and tucked his notebook away.

"I suppose I'll ride on back to Centennial Ridge. Got to send my follow-up story to the A.P." He held up his hands in surrender. "But don't worry. I'm a seasoned reporter with a great deal of respect for this doctor. She'll get a fair shake in my stories, always."

As much as Rebekah hated to admit it, having an influential newspaperman like Michael Hamilton in her corner was a blessing. She rose and offered to shake his hand. "Thank you, Mr. Hamilton. Please keep the story to a minimum."

He shook her hand stoutly and then held it a moment, looking her in the eyes. Then he grinned and released her hand, tipping his cockeyed derby hat.

"Good evening to you all."

Doctor McKinnon saw him to the door while Laramie tossed the pencil into the fireplace. Rebekah stared at the gray ash coating the broken pieces.

"It's all right, Lee. We can trust him."

Laramie held his jaw stiff as he glanced over his shoulder to the departing Michael Hamilton.

"I hope so."

# CHAPTER 4

The buggy ride into Centennial Ridge was a relief for Rebekah after being cooped up for six days. Doctor McKinnon had let her leave the ranch once, Sunday, to attend church surrounded by armed ranch hands. With the killer still at large, Laramie continued his vigilance of sleeping in the parlor of the ranch house.

Any window Rebekah looked out of or anywhere she went, someone watched her. While there was little chance of the killer being anywhere on the 50,000-acre ranch with all the hands on guard, Doctor McKinnon didn't want to take any chances. Whoever this man was, he was dangerous and had his sights set on Rebekah.

But there was a chance he'd never be caught, and Rebekah could not live in paralyzed fear.

Still, she didn't argue about Laramie Jones and Jimmy accompanying her on her shopping trip into Centennial Ridge. Jimmy asked her to drive the buggy while he kept a sharp eye out for a potential ambush. Laramie rode his gray horse Slate alongside the buggy, and she knew nothing escaped his attention.

When they arrived in Centennial Ridge, safe and sound, Rebekah heard Jimmy let out a big sigh.

"Feels good to breathe."

She smiled as she navigated traffic down Main Street to park the buggy in front of the millinery shop.

"You can breathe easy now, Jimmy. No one would dare try anything with so many witnesses around."

Jimmy shook his head as he set the buggy brake. "Don't know about that, ma'am. Senator Harris was stabbed right there in his office in the capitol building."

The chill Rebekah felt in the senator's office returned, but she shook it away. She had faced greater dangers than a shopping trip to Centennial Ridge.

Laramie dismounted and tied his big gray to a hitching post while Jimmy tied the buggy horse to another. Rebekah gathered her skirts and her medical bag, which she opted to carry instead of her reticule, and prepared to disembark.

Laramie was there, offering her a hand. She accepted it and climbed down, then realized her hand lingered in his. Whether it was because she hadn't pulled it away or he hadn't released it, she didn't want to know.

A few years ago, Rebekah had helped Laramie set up the ranch foreman cabin next to the bunkhouse when he'd been promoted. She'd taken a rug from Doctor McKinnon's attic and stretched it in front of the fireplace before he settled a rocking chair on it. He said the cabin had the makings of a real home.

Something about the way he spoke drove Rebekah to stay away from the McKinnon Ranch. She hurt Laramie Jones once, long ago, and she didn't want to again. She valued their friendship too much.

Rebekah swallowed, realizing she was staring up into Laramie's hazel eyes that almost matched the color of the sky today. She'd seen more of him this past week than she had in the months prior combined. It left her off balance when he wasn't right by her side. She didn't need that feeling of unbalance as she walked the path back to her people.

Laramie released her hand as Jimmy came around the buggy to reach for the bundle of letters behind the seat. "We going to the post office first, Miss Rebekah?"

She took a step back from Laramie. "Actually Jimmy, why don't you go on to the post office and mail my letters, too? I need to pick out some trade cloth. Laramie, Doctor McKinnon mentioned you would be visiting the '76 ranch and collecting money for a bull. You could do that while Jimmy and I finish here, then we'll ride home together."

Laramie lifted one eyebrow and the emotion in his eyes changed from what they were—she refused to call it love—to his guardian look.

"On one condition. You and Jimmy stick together here in town. I don't want you out of our sight."

Rebekah agreed to the compromise and Laramie remounted while she and Jimmy headed inside the millinery. After picking out two bolts of trade cloth and depositing them in the buggy, they headed for the post office.

Her bundle of letters was as thick as the entire ranch's combined. She spent most of her week writing letter after letter to anyone who might have influence for her cause, including a lengthy letter to the governor. After expressing her sorrow for Senator Harris's death, she listed everything she'd planned to say to the governor when they met.

She wrote each letter a half dozen times, but it wasn't until she handed them over to the postmaster that she made the actual decision to mail them. It took more courage than she thought. She hoped she didn't sound pleading in the letters, but she was— pleading for anyone to listen to her story and take up her cause.

As soon as they stepped onto the boardwalk again, a shriek, a yip, and a giggle greeted them.

"Miss Rebekah! Mr. Jimmy!"

Rebekah held her ground as the Palmer triplets and their dog, Valor, engulfed her and Jimmy. The triplets lived in town with their adoptive family now, after Jimmy rescued them from the Medicine Bow Mountains and their violent uncle Rufus.

The littlest Palmer, Roy, hooked one arm around Rebekah's waist and swung into her. He held tight, but didn't cling to her.

Roy pulled back, excitedly gesturing with his hands. He was going so fast and incorrectly that Rebekah couldn't make out the signs she'd taught him. She laughed and signed for him to slow down. Roy grinned from ear to ear as he made a fist and waved it up and down. His way of saying *yes*.

His sister Willie giggled; the only part of the girl Rebekah recognized at first. She was wearing a pink dress trimmed in lace and a frilly bonnet, her mousy brown hair done in curls down her back.

The "oldest," Wayne, wore a starched white shirt and a solemn face. But he looked proud as he watched his siblings and their black and white collie, Valor, who greeted Jimmy as robustly as the triplets.

"I told them we hadn't ought to bother you, Mr. Jimmy," Wayne said. "We're already going to be a bother when you take us to the circus on Friday, but, um, Valor really wanted to come and say howdy."

Jimmy scratched the dog behind her ears. "It's just Jimmy, remember? And it ain't no bother, is it, Miss Rebekah?"

His grin faded and he straightened. "Is it?"

While he looked the streets up and down as if suddenly remembering the threat they were under, Rebekah put her arm around Roy's shoulder and gave him a squeeze. "No bother at all. Perhaps the children would like to help us finish shopping."

Wayne shook his head. "The Robinsons told us to come right back. They're almost done picking up supplies at the general store. We just..."

Roy tugged on Rebekah's short navy jacket, then pointed

across the street. Willie voiced her brother's thoughts. "We wanted to show Mr. Jimmy the poster for the circus. They put them up all over town."

Jimmy looked to Rebekah who nodded her consent. He checked the streets again, his demeanor steady with the children as he said, "All right, let's take a look."

They made their way across the street to a post near the blacksmith shop. Roy pulled Rebekah ahead of the group as he pointed at the colorful illustrated posters nailed on the post.

She observed the fantastical land of the Donovan Brothers Circus—high flying, scantily-clad acrobats; clowns with faces covered with red, green and white paint; a fire-eating man. Fanciful script below a row of animals boasted of a "curious monster-eared African proboscidean marvel."

An elephant.

Jimmy stepped close to look at the poster below the main circus. He whistled low. "Say, Doc Beck, ain't this like the ticket you got a few months ago?"

Rebekah shifted her gaze to the illustrated poster that advertised the sideshow. It did match the ticket she'd nearly forgotten about—along with the disturbing fact that the legless man displayed in the illustration had his face covered with a thumbprint of blood.

Without that on this poster, Rebekah studied the man's face. A heavy beard and grudge makeup hid most of his features. It did give him an ape-like appearance, his fists balled and pressed on the ground, shoulders hunched forward.

There was something about the deep set of his eyes and the hook of his nose that filled Rebekah with a sense of familiarity. But she couldn't recall knowing him. She certainly hadn't attended a sideshow that exhibited his legless body.

Rebekah straightened. "It's the same, Jimmy, but I still have no idea why someone sent it."

She started to ask the triplets which part of the circus they most looked forward to, but a disturbance caught her attention. A man on horseback was flying high and fast on the road leading into town.

She recognized Slate and the straight way Laramie rode in the saddle, chaps flying.

Something was wrong.

She put her hand on the children's shoulders and directed them toward the general store. "You had best go on now, the Robinsons will be worried. Jimmy will come for you for the circus on Friday."

The triplets told Jimmy thank you again and by the time they and their dog were away, Laramie was sliding Slate to a deep stop in front of the blacksmith shop by Jimmy and Rebekah. Jimmy swung around.

Laramie spoke deep, urgent. "Get a move on, Jimmy, Becka, we're going back to the ranch. Now."

Rebekah lifted her skirts above her ankles to match Jimmy's long strides as they rushed to the buggy. She climbed aboard while he untied the horse.

Jumping into the seat beside her, he released the brake and slapped the reins across the horse's back, causing the mare to shoot out into a fast trot. He turned her head and slapped the reins again, sending her into a gallop out of town.

Laramie rode alongside them, looking behind, in front, to the left, and to the right. Jimmy focused on keeping the buggy on the road at the fastest clip the horse could take.

Rebekah clung to the arm of the buggy awning, medical bag situated in the seat between her and Jimmy. She could have her pepperbox out in seconds if needed.

What happened that was rushing them out of town?

Jimmy didn't slow the buggy even after they crossed under the MKR sign at the ranch entrance. They kept a steady and fast speed to the gravel road leading in front of Doctor McKinnon's home.

Their rushed entrance drew several of the hands to come running up the wide timbered steps on the hill from the corrals below.

Steve led the charge and called for two of the men to cool the horses down while Laramie dismounted and Jimmy helped Rebekah from the buggy. She was out of breath as though she had run from Centennial Ridge instead of the horse.

She directed her question at Laramie at the same time Steve and Jimmy did. "What happened?"

Laramie didn't answer, beckoning them to follow as he headed into the house.

Doctor McKinnon and Freddy met them in the foyer. Doctor McKinnon echoed the question. "What's happened?"

Laramie glanced between them and Rebekah let out a gasp. The sleeve of Laramie's left arm was soaked with blood.

# CHAPTER 5

Both doctors forced Laramie into the parlor and down on the sofa. He pushed back to his feet, holding up a hand to halt Rebekah's examination.

"I'm all right, it's just a graze. But I reckon it was meant to be more."

Rebekah froze, lost in the depths of Laramie's gray eyes. She moved her gaze to the blood on his sleeve. At least the bullet hadn't severed his brachial artery.

She swallowed, a flood of memories returning of the first time she had treated a very ill Laramie Jones. Or then, Private Lee Stafford. He'd been close to death and though she hardly knew him, her heart ached to save him.

Laramie looked to Steve and Jimmy. "Tell the boys to keep an eye out for a tall rider on a blue roan. I chased him, but he was too far ahead. He took a shot at me while I was on my way to the '76 outfit. I reckon he didn't know I was going out there soon enough to set up a good ambush."

Laramie gritted his teeth as though he hadn't meant to say the last part. Rebekah stared at him.

"You think it was the same man who killed Senator Jeffrey Harris, don't you? That...that he tried to kill you because of me?"

The room swirled. She was not the one in danger. It was those who meant the most to her.

❧

THE NEXT TWO days passed slowly as Rebekah remained inside the house, trying to fathom who would want to hurt her so much. She wrote out a list of possibilities, but it was short. Trying to make the pieces fit tired her mind and a feeling of panic settled in her soul.

Everyone she knew and loved was in danger because of her. How could she protect them all?

On the third morning, she went downstairs to take breakfast with Doctor McKinnon. Laramie Jones was at the table as well, holding his left arm stiff at his side. He still wouldn't wear the sling she'd given him. At least with him in the house, she'd been able to keep a close eye on the mild wound and change the bandage regularly.

The men rose at her entrance and Doctor McKinnon pulled out her chair to the right of his, across from Laramie.

Rebekah took it with a quiet *hó,* the expression for *thank you* in her people's language. It was all she could manage as she settled in, though her appetite rose with the aroma of cinnamon rolls coming from the kitchen. Freddy was at it again, making her favorite breakfast when he knew she'd be ready for comfort food.

Still, Rebekah found herself studying Laramie's left arm, unable to meet his eyes.

He said quietly, "It's healing fine, Becka."

She closed her eyes and when she opened them, Freddy had deposited two cinnamon rolls on her plate. She caught his dishwater-rough hand. "You are the best cook this house could have."

Freddy squinted with one eye, looking for all the world like Stubby, his twin brother.

"You don't say, Miss Becka? Even better than Stubs, you say?"

She wanted to laugh at his attempt to tease her into taking a side in their rivalry, but all she could muster was a small smile.

"I said, 'the house.' Stubby is the best in the bunkhouse. You are both best right where you are."

He accepted that with a scoff and went back to the kitchen.

The three ate in silence, and Rebekah waited until they finished to ask, "Is there any news from the Cheyenne marshal or Marshal Thorp?"

Doctor McKinnon leaned back and interlaced his fingers over his protruding waistline. "I'm afraid not. Whoever the murderer is, he made a clean break from Cheyenne."

"But Marshal Thorp has been told how Laramie was ambushed?"

Laramie answered, "I had a talk with Dave, and we scouted the area where I was shot. We found shells from the Buffalo gun he used, but no trail to follow. He plain vanished."

Rebekah took a sip of coffee, trying to hide her disappointment, though she wasn't surprised. Wyoming was a vast and rugged country, easily able to swallow one man who didn't want to be found.

# CHAPTER 6

The brass band shot thrills through Jimmy's heart. He tapped his toe to the beat of the drum, or at least tried as the band marched past in matching blue uniforms with white feather plumes on their hats.

No one could judge who was most enjoying the grand entry of the Donavan Brothers Circus into Centennial Ridge—him, the blackberry cobbler kids, or Valor.

He still thought of the triplets by the nickname he gave them, because they were sweet and kind of messy. And he loved blackberry cobbler.

All in his crew were grinning from ear to ear, waving at the clowns and acrobats who flipped, twirled, and juggled by. The excitement stirred everyone in Centennial Ridge and the surrounding area who gathered on Main Street to welcome the circus for their one-night performance.

Jimmy was determined to put aside the worry of the past week and make sure the triplets had a grand time. He might as well have a grand time, too.

Laramie Jones was at the ranch with other hands to guard Miss Rebekah, and Jimmy was allowed into town with the rest of the boys for the circus. Doc McKinnon gave them the time off to enjoy themselves.

Before leaving the ranch, he decided to wear the fringed jacket the former gunman, Cord Johnson, gave him. Jimmy hadn't worn it until then, because he didn't want to mess it up with work and it wasn't something he could wear to church. The circus was just the right occasion for it.

He figured they could all use some entertainment after being so intent on guarding Miss Rebekah, and now themselves after someone took a shot at Laramie Jones.

That rankled Jimmy something fierce, but he didn't reckon anything would happen to Laramie Jones. He was quite a man.

The parade ended with a gold and red Calliope wagon. Jimmy and the blackberry cobbler kids joined the other onlookers to trail the parade to the prairie grasslands outside of town. A red and white big top tent was set up along with a dozen other tents of all colors. Streamers and banners and posters marked the exhibits, sideshow, and carnival.

Steve, Lucky Saunders, and the other ranch hands scattered to the carnival games and food stands. Jimmy decided he could relax in this crowd of people, but he still needed to keep a sharp eye on the triplets.

He was solely responsible for the kids and that made him nervous. He nearly had to run to keep up with them as they bounced from exhibit to exhibit.

Miss Rebekah had given Jimmy extra money for the affair, but he still needed to be careful with their budget. Wayne wanted to do the shooting gallery and Roy made motions with his hands at a hawker selling balloons. Willie asked if they could all get rock candy and roasted peanuts.

Jimmy took off his hat and folded back one side of the lining to check the bills he had tucked there for buying tickets for the main show. He had the two tickets Miss Rebekah gave him for his birthday, and the kids were .25 cents each.

"All right, you each can pick two extra things..."

A hard slap on his shoulder sent him stumbling forward. Before he could turn around, he was engulfed by Lucky Saunders on one side and Steve on the other.

Lucky, his hand still on Jimmy's shoulder, gave him a shake that rattled his teeth and almost made him drop his hat.

"Aw, come on, Jimmy. A circus is no time for being cheap. I say we give them young'uns whatever they want."

Lucky reached into his vest pocket and retrieved a pouch that jingled. He tossed it at Willie, who caught it, her eyes round and gleeful.

Lucky waved his hand at the kids. "The boys pitched in to make sure y'all have the time of your lives. You too, Jimmy, and that's an order!"

He turned to Steve, who was flipping a silver dollar in the air and catching it. "Ain't that right, Mr. Temporary Foreman?"

Steve flipped the silver dollar again, this time straight at Jimmy's face. Jimmy caught it quick and Lucky and Steve laughed.

Steve said, "As long as you're wearing that old gunman's jacket, I reckon you better have yourself a time, too."

Jimmy stared dumbfounded at his friends who grinned and strode off.

Willie squealed and Roy hopped in place while Wayne grimly nodded as though having a grand time was going to be serious work. He eyed Jimmy.

"That all right, Just Jimmy? Can we really spend whatever's in that bag?"

Jimmy held his hand out and Willie reluctantly surrendered the bag. Jimmy rubbed it between his fingers, feeling the coins inside. Then he handed it back to Willie.

"The Good Book says its more blessed to give than receive. I reckon it will bring the boys a lot of pleasure, seeing you three spend that money."

Roy plowed into Jimmy, giving him a big hug before dashing off with his siblings for the balloon vendor.

Jimmy ambled after them, thinking about the friends he'd made on McKinnon Ranch. Now if he could just talk them all into getting baptized with him.

# CHAPTER 7

The circus was more fun than Jimmy even dreamed. The flying acrobats, clowns, real live elephants—the largest creatures Jimmy had ever seen—dogs that rode on ponies' backs. Best of all, was watching the blackberry cobbler kids eat it up like it was the greatest thing they'd ever seen or ever would see in their lifetimes.

For the vast prairieland rivers, mountains, and natural beauty of Wyoming, it could be a desolate place with little fanfare. A circus like this gave people a chance to get out and laugh and make memories that would last long into their lifetime. Jimmy sure hoped so with the kids. It was making memories for him, especially watching the kids and the other ranch hands who enjoy the show with them.

Anticipation built for the grand finale, something the circus ringmaster really played up. He quieted the crowd in the steaming, sawdust-smelling big top as he stood in the center ring, turning in a slow circle. His black tailcoat and red vest made him look as tall as a tree, even when he swept his top hat off to address the crowd.

"Ladies and gentlemen, you are about to witness a feat that defies..."

He made a swift rotation and landed with one foot extended. He locked eyes with the crowd. Jimmy could've sworn he made direct eye contact with him as he emphasized the final word.

"*Death.*"

The audience applauded, but the ringmaster wouldn't let Jimmy go with his eyes. Movement at the back entrance caught everyone else's attention and the ringmaster finally turned to introduce the human cannonball.

Jimmy gulped, wondering at the cold sweat on his forehead. That ringmaster was a powerful man.

As soon as the show was over, Jimmy herded the triplets out of the big top. The outside was lit with torches and laughter. The circus wasn't over yet. Every vendor was ready to draw in the crowd to their stands and exhibits.

As they stood in line for more roasted peanuts, Willie asked him, "How come Doc Beck didn't come?"

Jimmy shrugged. "She told me she's not much for circuses, but she wanted us to all have a good time."

Wayne shoved his hands in his pockets. "She's a very nice lady. How come she's an old maid?"

Jimmy felt his eyes pop wide, remembering the time he sort-of suggested Miss Rebekah was old enough to be his mother. "That's a im-po-lite question, Wayne."

Jimmy carefully sounded out the word. Miss Rebekah used it so often with him, and he wanted to try it out himself.

They got their peanuts and Roy tugged on the fringed jacket to get Jimmy's attention. He pointed to the one tent Jimmy had steered them away from—the sideshow.

Jimmy was still uneasy about the bizarre ticket someone sent to Miss Rebekah. But Roy looked like he really wanted to go. Maybe he wanted to see if there were people who were different like him.

If Jimmy needed more convincing, someone pushed him from behind. It was Lucky Saunders.

"Hey Jimmy, you know there's a scientist fella that said we evolved from monkeys? Maybe this ape man is one of our ancestors."

Wayne looked up at Lucky, his face illuminated by one of the torches. "What's 'evolve' mean?"

Lucky scratched the back of his head, pushing his hat forward. "Well, if that fella is right, it means we started out as monkeys millions of years ago, and then gradually stood up straighter and lost most of that hair and became what we are."

Wayne frowned. "So monkeys are still becoming men somewhere in the world?"

Lucky opened his mouth, but nothing came out. He pulled out a silver dollar. "I'm buying."

Jimmy reluctantly trailed Lucky and the kids into the sideshow.

It was dim and quiet inside that tent. A man dressed in an ill-fitting gray suit, orange vest unbuttoned, and no hat stood before the small crowd gathering for a tour. He sure wasn't as flashy and captivating as the ringmaster.

The plump man gestured awkwardly with his hands. "And here, women, er, ladies, and gentlemen, are two people in one. Twins that never got apart from each other. Meet Barney and Arnie."

Everyone was transfixed on the man's stumbling speech, including Jimmy, but then gasps echoed in the tent.

He turned and saw a sight that struck him dumb. One man sat in a chair, but he had two heads!

Jimmy blinked, thinking the heads would merge into one. But they didn't, faces turned to the ground. Jimmy couldn't stop staring even after the group moved on. He took a tentative step forward and one of the heads looked up at him.

Jimmy whispered, "You all right?"

The other head looked at him and its expression was different. This was two men, not one. Barney and Arnie.

The first one's eyes clouded over, but the other one snapped, "Move along."

Jimmy stepped back and joined the rest of the spectators.

The next exhibit was a man he'd seen earlier, throwing fire with his breath. Only now he was swallowing a sword, cutting right through his innards as he took the whole thing down his mouth.

Jimmy could hardly watch, but he didn't want those twins to catch him staring at them again, so he focused on the disappearing sword.

At the next exhibit, the man with the ill-fitting suit explained, was the smallest woman in the world. Jimmy wouldn't doubt it. If the little lady was next to him, she'd hardly come up to his gun belt.

Then the group moved to the final display. A huge red drape covered something that stood in the corner of the tent. The man in the gray and orange suit waved his hands over his head, trying to be dramatic.

"You folks, get prepared for an amazing sight. Never before seen in Wyoming, is this here ape that looks like a man. I mean, this here man that acts like an ape. Brought from the wilds of Brazil, or one of those South American countries, all the way here to astonish you tonight."

He grabbed the drape with both hands and said over his shoulder, "I give you—the Ape Man!"

He yanked the heavy drape away to reveal a cage as high as Jimmy's head. People gasped and took a step back, allowing Jimmy a clear view.

There he was, the ape man from the bloody ticket Miss Rebekah refused to use.

# CHAPTER 8

It was getting late in the evening, but after Jimmy took the blackberry cobbler kids home, he found none of the hands were inclined to head back to the ranch. They had the night off and wanted to make the most of it. Since none of them were supposed to ride back alone, Jimmy was stuck.

But he was as hungry as they were. The McKinnon outfit converged on the hotel restaurant for a late-night meal. The restaurant was open to accommodate post-circus goers, and the ranch hands weren't the only ones. They had to wait for tables.

Jimmy found a spot in the lobby to wait near Stubby and Freddy, who were arguing about Freddy's cinnamon roll recipe. Freddy had a special ingredient he used and refused to give it away, even to his own brother. Stubby railed that he made meals that stuck to one's ribs while Freddy spent too much time on the sweet tooth.

From the hollering, Jimmy was afraid they might come to blows, but he learned in his time at the ranch that the brothers were scarcely serious in their cantankerous ways. As long as they didn't get really and truly riled.

That didn't happen. Instead, they challenged each other to a cook off and buffaloed their way into the hotel kitchen to make cinnamon rolls, much to the delight of the McKinnon ranch hands. Most of them, at least.

As they snagged tables one by one, Jimmy noticed some of the boys were missing, including Steve and Lucky. He felt a tinge of worry, especially for Steve since he and Miss Rebekah were good buddies.

But wherever Steve was, Lucky Saunders and the others were. Jimmy couldn't worry over every little thing.

As the restaurant emptied of families and couples, Stubby and Freddy served cinnamon rolls to the ranch hands and the restaurant staff, who appreciated it after the long day.

Jimmy pitched in to help clean up the kitchen with the brothers, and when it was finally time to go, Jimmy snagged Stubby's arm.

"Do you know where Lucky and Steve are?"

Stubby snorted. "What kind of fool question is that? We're in town on a Friday night."

Jimmy stared at him and Stubby's cantankerousness faded. He shook his head. "Just get ready to ride out with us. The rest of them will find their way back by morning."

Jimmy started to ask another question, fool or not, when the same hard slap he'd gotten earlier struck him on the shoulder.

Lucky gave him a shake. "Jimmy boy, I come to fetch you to have some real fun. You don't want to ride back with these old men, do you?"

Now that Jimmy took an inventory, he realized that most of the hands who had stayed at the restaurant were among the older, churchgoing lot of the McKinnon hands.

"I reckon I'll ride on back, Lucky. I—"

"Don't be an old granny." Lucky thumped Jimmy in the chest with the back of his hand. "You had to be a babysitter all day. Well, you're a man and you ought to have some man-sized fun. There's a new machine down the street that I want to show you."

Jimmy glanced between him and Stubby, Lucky with his big grin and Stubby staring them both down, hands on his hips.

One thing Jimmy knew, these older cowhands would be at church Sunday morning. The ones with Lucky Saunders—may or may not be. Did the Lord want Jimmy to nudge them along?

Jimmy said to Stubby, "I reckon I'll be coming home with Lucky and the others."

Stubby shook his head, swinging his hands off his hips as he turned and headed out the back door.

Lucky pulled Jimmy out of the hotel and down Main Street. He slung one arm around Jimmy's shoulder and started to sing.

*In a cavern, in a canyon*
*Excavating for a mine*
*Dwelt a miner, forty-niner*
*And his daughter, Clementine*

*Oh my darling, oh my darling*
*Oh my darling, Clementine*
*You are lost and gone forever*
*Dreadful sorry, Clementine*

His loud pitch and off-key notes told Jimmy that Lucky had already been drinking, and he was now steering them straight for the saloon.

Lucky used his free fist to hit the swinging doors as he dragged Jimmy inside. The room smelled like smoke and beer and cheap perfume, and Jimmy knew he had ought to skedaddle out of there.

Lucky, his arm still hooked around Jimmy's neck, dragged him over to the bar. He slapped his palm on it and spoke to the bartender. "Set 'em up for me and my friend."

Jimmy shook his head. "You know I don't drink."

"I know that, and I ain't here to corrupt you." Lucky released Jimmy. "I'm going to drink for both of us!"

The bartender set two foaming mugs in front of them. Lucky picked them up, clinked them together, and took a big gulp of both at the same time.

Jimmy scooted out of the path of the sloshing beer. Shaking his head, he turned his gaze to roam the tables, looking for Steve.

A man banged on a piano in the back corner. Cowhands gambled, saloon girls lounged with the free-spending men who, like the McKinnon hands, had gotten the night off for the circus. Jimmy even saw a few circus people, still half in costume. He shouldn't have worn his fringed jacket into the saloon. There were a few men who eyed Jimmy like they were looking for a fight.

But he didn't see Steve.

A bolt of fear went through Jimmy. He quickly turned back to Lucky, his elbow catching the mug in the man's hand and knocking it to the floor.

Lucky cussed him, but Jimmy talked louder. "Where's Steve? He wasn't with the others and he's not here. He could be in trouble."

Lucky guffawed and picked up the other foaming mug. He put it to his lips, chuckling into it.

"Don't you worry about Steve. He can take care of himself. Now come on, try out this machine."

Lucky prodded Jimmy to the other end of the bar. The machine sitting there was a square box with a glass front that showed an arrangement of wooden pegs that descended down into one of several holes at the bottom.

Lucky dug into his vest pocket and produced a nickel that he pressed in Jimmy's hand.

"Here, drop this in and see which slot it lands in."

Jimmy sighed. He wasn't in the mood for games, but maybe if he went along with Lucky awhile, he could find out where Steve was.

Jimmy chose a center hole at the top of the machine to drop the nickel in. The coin bounced down the pegs, pinging to one side and then the other. It bounced down and dropped into one of the slots at the bottom.

Lucky hooted. "By thunder, you did it, Jimmy! Made back five times the bet."

He called to the bartender, "Set 'em up again!"

A man standing behind the bar paid out five nickels to Jimmy. He stared at them, dumbfounded.

"Lucky Saunders, did you just get me to gamble?"

"Ain't gambling if it's someone else's money, is it?" Lucky swiped the nickels from Jimmy.

Jimmy rubbed a hand over his face, wanting to block out the sounds and smell of the saloon, and worse, what he'd just done. He didn't gamble, didn't cuss, and here Lucky was about to have him doing both.

Jimmy turned away from the machine, staring across the room at the staircase leading to the second floor. He slouched back against the bar as Lucky dropped a nickel in the machine. Jimmy could hear it striking the pegs and then Lucky groaned before dropping another nickel in.

Jimmy shook his head. He shouldn't be there. If he left now, he could catch up with Stubby and the others...

Movement at the top of the stairs caught his attention along with a familiar gray shirt and yellow bandanna.

Jimmy stared as Steve descended the stairs, one of the saloon girls hanging on his friend's arm. Steve had his hat in hand, talking to the girl who then looked past him and met Jimmy's eyes.

Her look was inviting, and Jimmy froze. Steve turned to see what had her attention and came to a dead halt when he spotted Jimmy.

Lucky rolled around, hooking his elbows on the bar behind him as he looked at Jimmy and then over to the staircase.

Lucky whistled loud. "Now, Steve, is that what you want to be doing when the Lord comes back?"

Jimmy wasn't sure what was making his face burn more—the girl's look, Steve's embarrassment, or his own anger. He pushed away from the bar and headed for the swinging doors of the saloon.

Steve shouted after him, "You can't be riding back alone, Jimmy!"

Jimmy ignored him. There was sure nothing more dangerous for him between town and the ranch than inside that saloon.

# CHAPTER 9

Jimmy never used spurs on his Kate, but he was sorely tempted to that night. Anything to get out of town fast and caught up with the other McKinnon ranch hands. But Kate was plenty fast without spurs and Jimmy streaked by the circus camp where the crew was tearing down to move to the next town.

Jimmy galloped away from one of the best nights of his life—until Lucky Saunders hauled him into that saloon. Jimmy didn't know what to do about him and Steve, he only knew he had to get back to the ranch himself. A saloon was no place for young men of weak or strong character. Jimmy couldn't honestly say which he was right then.

The other hands couldn't have much of a head start on him and wouldn't be riding near as fast as Jimmy on the dark road. Still, he cut through a draw and dense underbrush to climb a rise to the west side of the road. On the east side of the rise lay the Little Medicine Bow River.

He'd likely be able to see the crew from the top of the rise. Wyoming miles were long miles. Jimmy let Kate climb the steep rise at her own pace and they soon reached the top.

There, not more than a mile ahead, a group of riders were loping for McKinnon Ranch. Jimmy would catch up with them soon.

But another sight caught his attention to the east. A lone rider was trotting in the opposite direction, toward the Little Medicine Bow River. Jimmy watched the rider, blinking to clear his vision against the full moon reflecting on the prairie grass and river far below.

There was something strange about the way the man sat the saddle. Then Jimmy realized what had caught his attention.

The man was riding a blue roan.

*A blue roan.* The man who shot Laramie rode a blue roan.

Not that there was only one in Wyoming, but there was as good a chance as any that it was this one. A lone rider in the dark had to be up to no good.

As soon as the thought came to mind, Jimmy chided himself. He was a lone rider out in the dark and it wasn't because he was up to no good.

Still, he nudged Kate to cross the road to the edge of the rise, willing his eyes to see better, to determine what was so odd about this rider.

The man pulled up by the river and swung off the horse. Jimmy immediately knew what was so strange.

The man had no legs.

## CHAPTER 10

Rebekah thought to sleep in Saturday morning, but something jolted her, and she sat upright at dawn. She remained still in the bed, trying to comprehend the sense of foreboding that overcame her.

She realized two things. One, most of the ranch hands went into the circus last night. Laramie had taken a watch on the front porch with a rifle in his arms and she knew he would be there until the last cowhand was in. Had they all made it back?

Second, the aroma of bacon cooking was absent. Even on Saturdays, Freddy felt it was shameful if breakfast wasn't ready before dawn.

Rebekah quickly dressed. She wanted to see if Laramie was still on the porch.

Downstairs, the smell of coffee greeted her, relieving some of her tension. She glanced into the empty parlor, then crossed the foyer to the front door.

The misty morning of the Wyoming prairieland greeted her, along with Doctor McKinnon and Laramie Jones. They stood from rocking chairs on the porch, the creaks old and familiar.

Doctor McKinnon offered to get Rebekah a cup of coffee,

which she declined for the moment and addressed Laramie. He looked like coffee was the only thing keeping his eyes open.

"Did everyone come in last night?"

Laramie took a sip, the movement of his arm natural. His wound was healing well. "Not quite. I'm going to ride in this morning and knock some heads together."

"Not alone." The words rushed so quickly out of Rebekah's mouth, she wasn't surprised at the measured look Laramie gave her. She spoke like he was a child instead of a man who always knew what he was doing.

She sighed and turned to Doctor McKinnon, who handed her his coffee cup of fine bone china. She sipped a tiny bit.

"I'm sorry. I just woke up all jittery, thinking about how everyone is in danger, and it's my fault."

Laramie stepped to the side, allowing Rebekah to sit in one of the rockers. She felt exhausted. Perched on the edge of the rocker, she glanced down at the barnyard, tense all over.

"Maybe you could take Jimmy with you?" It was her way of asking if her young friend was safe.

Laramie answered quietly, "I figured to let him sleep. He came in pretty late."

Rebekah closed her eyes, relieved. "I suppose you could have breakfast first. At least Freddy already has coffee going."

Doctor McKinnon shifted, pulling his watch out of his pocket and checking it. "Actually, I put the coffee on this morning."

The clouds in Laramie's eyes made Rebekah cold all over. "Freddy's not in the kitchen?" Laramie asked. "Stubby came in last night, I figured Freddy was with..."

Laramie didn't finish, setting his coffee cup aside and reaching for his rifle leaned against the wall. Rebekah looked to see what had caught Laramie's attention.

Two riders were coming up the road, headed for the ranch house at a steady trot. They looked like they were in a hurry, yet at the same time, dreaded where they were going.

Laramie recognized the men before Rebekah did. He leaned the rifle against one of the round columns before going down the steps, Doctor McKinnon behind him.

Rebekah couldn't move from her perch on the rocking chair as she watched the men approach. When they were close enough, she recognized Lucky Saunders and another hand. The other hand went left at the split in the road, heading for the barnyard and bunkhouse.

Lucky Saunders turned right, up the short road that ran in front of the McKinnon house. He pulled to a stop by the hitching post as Doctor McKinnon and Laramie met him.

Rebekah slowly rose from the rocker and went down the steps. She'd never seen Lucky's face so tight, like his throat was closed up. He met her eyes and then looked away.

His voice was low, but she could still hear him say to Laramie, "Bad news, boss. Real bad. I'm awful sorry."

The last part he mumbled, and Rebekah edged closer. She could see his eyes were red and swollen. He looked like he had a severe hangover.

Laramie spoke, his voice calm and controlled enough to instill courage in his men whether in the cavalry or on a ranch. "Tell me what happened, Lucky."

The cowhand leaned over the saddle, resting his arms on the horn. He stared at the reins in his hands.

"Marshal Thorp come to get us at the, well, several of the boys stayed the night in town. Steve sent me to fetch you…"

"Go on, Lucky."

Lucky's reddened eyes met Rebekah's again. "It's Freddy. They found him near a circus concession, stabbed dead."

CHAPTER 11

Rebekah was numb as Doctor McKinnon drove the buggy to Centennial Ridge. A caravan went before and behind the buggy, made up of McKinnon ranch hands, including Laramie Jones, Jimmy, and Stubby Goodman.

Before they rode out, one of the men explained how Freddy stopped off at the circus, saying he wanted to talk to the candy butcher again, trying to convince him to show Freddy how to make a new invention called cotton candy. Freddy said he'd ride back to the ranch with the other crew.

Stubby took the news of his brother's death stoically as he rode at the front of the procession that felt like a funeral march to Rebekah. This was the first time she'd seen Jimmy really cry.

Her own tears hadn't come yet, couldn't until she found out what happened, who was responsible, and see them brought to justice.

That was on the mind of every McKinnon ranch hand.

Near town, Rebekah got her first glimpse of the Donovan Brothers Circus. Odd that they were erecting the big top tent instead of tearing it down.

She was too dazed to pay much attention to it, but the fact

47

that this was where Freddy was found had her staring at every face staring back at her. Suspicion ebbed mutually between them.

The McKinnon crew went straight to the marshal's office. Rebekah couldn't help but feel relieved to see the rest of the McKinnon ranch hands hanging around on the front porch. Steve stood leaning against one post. He looked up, his fresh young face drawn and tired.

Doctor McKinnon handed Rebekah down from the buggy and they went into the marshal's office, trailed by Laramie. And Stubby.

Stubby marched to the other door that opened into the jail cells while Doctor McKinnon and Rebekah approached Marshal Thorp.

He rose from behind his desk and nodded solemnly. "I'm real sorry, Doc McKinnon." He met Rebekah's eyes. "Doctor Anderson wanted to know if you wanted to assist with the autopsy, Miss Becka. He'd welcome your expertise."

Marshal Thorp faltered at the end, probably from the stricken look Rebekah gave him. She could not possibly dissect someone she'd known and loved.

Stubby stomped out from the cells and barked, "I don't see no one behind bars for murder."

Marshal Thorp sighed. "I don't have anyone to arrest yet. I did tell those circus people not to leave town. They kicked up a pretty good fuss, but the ringmaster, Calvin Blackthorn, settled them and said they'd put on another show tonight. It could have been one of them, could have not. I need to ask...did Freddy have any enemies, anyone who would—"

Stubby banged a fist on the desk. "He was gentle as a lamb!"

Marshal Thorp gave him a sidelong look, his gaze turning steely. "Folks at the restaurant said you and he were having a rounder last night."

Before Stubby could explode, Doctor McKinnon said, "You know better than that, Dave."

The marshal dragged a hand over his face, then picked up a piece of paper from his desk. He held it out to Doctor McKinnon, who read it aloud.

"*Are brothers forever?*"

Marshal Thorp pointed at the note. "We found that near Freddy last night." He glanced at Stubby again. "I was hoping maybe you could tell us what it meant."

Laramie cut in, "There was an ominous note found with Senator Jeffrey Harris' body, too. It was typed, but…" He halted. Rebekah went cold all over.

Senator Harris. The ambush on Laramie. Freddy's death.

They were all connected…because of her.

She felt herself losing her balance and Doctor McKinnon took hold of her elbow.

*No.* Freddy's death could not be because of her.

The marshal's office door opened, and Rebekah expected to see one of the ranch hands, but it admitted Michael Hamilton instead.

He swept off his hat like he was ready to launch into his usual litany of questions, until he saw Rebekah and the others.

He came slowly forward, nodding at her. "I'm very sorry for your loss. I know something like this hits a crew hard."

Rebekah received his sympathy with a nod. As long as he was not pounding her with questions, she could be civil with Michael Hamilton.

Hamilton turned to the marshal. "I just came to ask a few follow-up questions, Marshal Thorp. They can wait."

Laramie turned to the marshal. "Speaking of questions, did you talk to everyone in that circus?"

Marshal Thorp nodded. "I did, but not hardly a one talked back to me. Said they didn't hear or see anything, though it's hard to believe no one in that camp knows anything about how a dead man got in the midst of them."

The marshal winced, as though just remembering the dead man was near to the hearts of those in his office.

Rebekah glanced at Doctor McKinnon and Laramie, then held her hand out for the note. "Maybe it's time the crew of the McKinnon Ranch asked a few questions of our own."

# CHAPTER 12

Though Doctor McKinnon ordered most of the ranch hands to stay behind—he didn't want any violent clashes—it was still a contingent that strode out to the circus camp.

Doctor McKinnon and Laramie led the way, Rebekah between them. Stubby, Jimmy, Steve, and Lucky followed behind, along with Michael Hamilton, tablet in hand.

Rebekah noticed he had been taking quite a few notes, and every word worried her. She wished he would stop writing about her.

There hadn't been enough time to receive responses to her letters, but that mattered little right then. Rebekah couldn't take this trouble home to her people.

They started at the concession where Freddy was found, but the candy butcher had no more to say to them than he had in divulging his recipes.

They visited other tents and knocked on the door of the circus manager's wagon, but there was no answer.

Jimmy tapped Rebekah's arm. She turned to find him angling

his head toward a yellow and red striped tent where a plump man hammered spikes to hold the tent up.

"That's the tent for the sideshow, ma'am. We went in last night and saw the ape man. But that ain't the only time I saw him." He looked up at Laramie. "I was going to tell you about it last night, but…"

Jimmy's eyes flickered toward Steve and he frowned. "I just wanted to get on to bed. Figured to tell you this morning, but when I was riding back last night, I seen a man riding toward the Little Medicine Bow River. When he got off his horse, I saw it was the ape man. He was riding a blue roan."

Laramie's eyes flashed and he jerked around to stare at the tent. "We know who to question next."

They approached the yellow and red tent where the man finished striking the last spike. He straightened and turned, hammer in hand. On seeing the small crowd near the door, he growled, "Show's not till tonight. You'll have to get your tickets then."

From his inner coat pocket, Doctor McKinnon withdrew what Rebekah recognized as the sideshow ticket someone sent her months ago. He held it up, the bloody thumbprint over the man's face flashing in the sunlight. "We already have a ticket, sir. We'd like to see this man."

The plump man's face reddened and he snapped, "Look, I'm just the temporary sideshow manager. I don't know nothin' about nothin'."

Michael Hamilton stepped forward and began asking questions in his style that wouldn't let his subject get away until he answered them all.

But Rebekah's attention was drawn away by Jimmy tugging on her elbow. He beckoned her to the corner of the tent. She glanced back and caught Laramie's eye. He separated from the group to follow them.

Rebekah spotted where Jimmy was taking her: A tent with an

open face set up, a variety of people under its shade doing a variety of projects—cooking over an open fire, sewing ripped costumes, polishing oversized clown shoes.

Seated near the edge of the opening were dicephalic parapagus twins, each reading a different book. Rebekah had studied this type of rare case in medical school, but this was the first time she had seen a living pair. Surely Jimmy didn't want her to come and gape at them?

One of the twins looked up and scowled. "Show isn't until tonight."

The other twin lowered his book, and Jimmy spoke up. "Miss Rebekah, this is Barney and Arnie. Fellows, I come to apologize for gawking at…at you boys last night. It was mean."

The first one asked, "What are you sorry for? That's what we're here for."

Jimmy glanced at Rebekah and she nodded encouragement. He hooked his thumbs in his gun belt. "But do you want to be, Arnie?"

The scowling one frowned deep while the other looked taken aback. Rebekah wondered how often spectators actually spoke to them as if they were human beings.

The second one said quietly, "I'm Arnie. Arnold. He's Bernard."

Jimmy nodded. "I'm just Jimmy."

Bernard grumbled, "Move along. We got nothing to say about your friend. We were in bed asleep when it happened."

Rebekah shifted to leave, but Jimmy wasn't finished. He squatted so he was eye level with Arnold and Bernard.

"You know something? Our friend, the one who died, he has a twin brother. Stubby." His voice caught. "Stubby and Freddy."

Arnold glanced at Bernard, then back at Jimmy before saying quietly, "Not all of us were asleep last night."

Bernard snapped, "Keep quiet. "

Arnold hesitated, then pressed in. "I think that man is a little crazy."

"So do I, but I think quiet."

Rebekah furrowed her brows. "What man?"

Arnold opened his mouth to answer, but Bernard clamped a hand over it and gave Rebekah a hard look.

"I said, *move along*. Stay away from freaks from now on."

# CHAPTER 13

The parlor was deathly quiet that evening. Disturbingly so. Rebekah sat in there alone and she was both grateful and regretful of it.

One of the hands was on the front porch, standing guard, while Laramie worked in the kitchen to bake some sort of dessert—not Stubby's specialty. The bunkhouse cook headed to his quarters after insisting on preparing dinner for the house. Doctor McKinnon took up residence in his study to write long-overdue correspondence.

Rebekah didn't know whether to join her uncle or Laramie, so she settled in the parlor with bright red trade cloth to sew shirts for distant relations on the Omaha Indian Reservation. She mailed shirts annually so the children would have a new one to start the school year in the fall.

The repetitive stitches soothed her even as her heart ached for all the love and loss in her life.

Soon after the clock chimed 8PM, the front door opened, and the ranch hand called for Laramie.

Rebekah stilled, watching the foyer, holding her breath as Laramie strode through it, large white apron protecting his shirt and trousers from the flour bin. But the apron didn't fully conceal the six-gun he wore. Stubby always wore his six-gun when cooking, only he wore it on the outside of his apron.

There was murmuring at the doorway and Laramie took a step back to look in on Rebekah with a frown. She rose as a boisterous voice from the driveway reached her.

"Hello the house! Hold your fire, I'm friendly."

Michael Hamilton. No wonder Laramie was frowning. Rebekah laid aside her sewing project.

She saw the exchange between the two men as Hamilton entered and sidestepped Laramie, giving him and the apron a long look.

Rebekah called, "Come in, Mr. Hamilton."

Michael Hamilton removed his derby hat and greeted her with a dim smile. "Good evening, my dear Doc Beck. I've come with both answers and questions, if I may."

Rebekah gestured to the sofa while she took the armchair.

Hamilton seated himself. "First, the answers. I have written down every fact about these cases and discovered new ones. You recall telling me about the touchy sideshow manager you encountered this afternoon?"

"Yes."

"Well, it seems he was made manager just a week ago, when the prior manager, Will Flit, was found stabbed in the sideshow tent the night before the circus performance in Cheyenne."

Rebekah pressed her hand against her throat. Hamilton continued.

"The deed was done with a large knife, similar to the one used on Senator Harris. Neither knife was found. Now, for my questions. I cannot, for the life of me, connect the two Cheyenne murders and your dear cook, Freddy. But you were among those who found Senator Harris. If we go through every detail from the moment you arrived in Cheyenne until..."

Rebekah closed her eyes, not wanting to recall examining the senator's body. She went further back to their arrival at the state capitol building. They'd taken seats outside the senator's office to wait, and eventually Doctor McKinnon went downstairs to seek the senator or his assistant. He returned, and Stanley Cook went straight to the door and...

Rebekah's eyes flew open. "Why did he assume the door was locked?"

Michael Hamilton raised his eyebrows and flipped his tablet to a blank page. "Who?"

"If Stanley Cook thought the senator was inside, why would the door be locked? There was no reason for the senator to lock the door from the inside. People are allowed to wait in the office area when they're coming to see a senator, aren't they?"

Michael Hamilton stared at her. "That's what I've experienced, and I've been in plenty of those offices for interviews. Perhaps I should make a trip to Cheyenne and have a talk with that assistant."

Rebekah shook her head. "I can't imagine what his connection would be to the circus, nor why he would harm the senator."

Hamilton tapped a beat on his tablet. "Well now, Doc Beck, that's why you have me. I'm not just your run-of-the-mill reporter. I investigate until I get every scrap of the story I can. Just like you did when you performed the autopsy down there at Hagan, New Mexico, and pinned the murder on the right killer."

Rebekah looked to the cold fireplace and rubbed her arms. She was grieved enough without reminders of that tragedy.

Michael Hamilton tossed his tablet on the tea table and scooted forward to kneel in front of her chair. He encased her cold hands in his warm ones.

"Now, now, Miss Rebekah. Nothing will happen to you here. You've got an awful lot of men around who would shoot anyone who gave you a wrong look."

Rebekah tugged on her hands, but Michael Hamilton patted them, meeting her eyes. He sighed deep.

"If I'm ever gonna say this, I might as well now. You are one fantastic woman, Doctor Rebekah LaRoche. I would turn a cartwheel if you allowed me to court you when we're in the same area; could be often if we tried."

Rebekah gave a soft laugh and squeezed his hand in return. "Mr. Hamilton, I think we'd best stick to the professions we both do well."

Michael Hamilton sighed again, long and dramatic. "It's because of Laramie Jones, isn't it? I can recognize a rival when I meet one."

Rebekah shifted back in the chair, pulling away from him in earnest. He released her hands and she stammered, "I—Laramie is a special friend, but..."

"Too special at times, eh, Miss Rebekah? Is that why you don't anchor in one place for very long?"

A loud rap sounded at the parlor entrance and Rebekah jerked to see Laramie standing there, a frown etched through the worn creases of his face, apron and boots dusted with flour. He stared at the man on one knee in front of Rebekah.

"You want this fellow to leave, Miss Becka?"

Hamilton stood, giving his vest a stout tug to straighten it. "If the lady had asked me to leave, I wouldn't be here." He eyed the apron. "You do make a fine nursemaid."

Laramie reached behind him and snapped the apron string loose. He pulled the cloth over his head and tossed it aside. Despite the streak of flour across the bridge of his nose, he looked for all the world like the day he was promoted to army captain.

Rebekah said quietly, "Mr. Hamilton, Laramie Jones is my oldest and truest friend."

Laramie hooked his thumbs in his gun belt, staring at Michael Hamilton. "You'd do best to remember that."

Laramie glanced at Rebekah, and she knew it was she who truly needed to remember it.

# CHAPTER 14

There was never a duller Saturday night in the history of ranch work.

But Steve couldn't bring himself to feel bad for that as he sat slouched at the round card table in the bunkhouse. He stared at his cards that made no more sense than Freddy's death. He thumbed one corner of his five-card hand, thinking about a lot of things; thinking about nothing.

Lucky rapped his knuckles on the table across from Steve. Steve eyed his friend over the top of his cards.

Lucky drawled, "If I have to ask you one more time if you're in or folding, I'm dealing you out of the next hand."

Steve sighed and glanced at his cards—a pair of eights and a pair of threes. He tossed three matchsticks to the center of the table.

"I'll call you."

Lucky sighed, agitated. None of the boys were in a joking mood tonight.

"Henderson is the one you're calling, not me, you oaf."

Steve shifted, pushing himself up a little and preparing to lay his cards on the table. "You, Henderson, that newspaper reporter; what difference does it make?"

Before he could lay his cards out, a distant shout echoed from outside, and Steve was sure he recognized the voice. He took a quick glance around the bunkhouse, remembering he was temporary foreman.

"Where's Jimmy?"

A hand lounging on the cot below Jimmy's spoke up. "He said he was going to talk to the horses, or something. You know how he is. Makes a good head wrangler. No offense, Steve."

Piercing whinnies came from the corral down and across from the bunkhouse. It sounded like the horses were in a terrible tizzy.

Steve flung his cards to the table. "No one's supposed to be alone!"

He shoved his chair back, toppling it, and darted for the door, Lucky behind him.

Steve threw open the door and called back to the other hands, "No one by themselves, you hear?"

He stumbled onto the porch of the bunkhouse, his gaze swiveling and landing on the corral. In the dark, Steve couldn't make out much, but he could see the gate, wide open, and horses charging through.

He ran hard for the corral, but too late to stop any of them from fleeing. He shouted at the boys coming out of the bunkhouse, "That's half the remuda! Saddle up and get them rounded up!"

Out of breath, Steve doubled over at the corral gate, resting his hands on his knees. Lucky gasped for air beside him. Then Lucky gripped Steve's arm.

"Steve."

Lucky sounded like he was strangling on his own tongue.

Still doubled over, Steve looked sideways into the corral. Laying in the middle of it, face down, was Jimmy.

# CHAPTER 15

Before Rebekah could defuse the tension between Laramie Jones and Michael Hamilton, a gunshot shattered the night.

Laramie was the first to the door, Rebekah behind him. He flashed out a hand to hold her back, but then dropped it. He understood she wasn't staying behind.

Doctor McKinnon rushed from his study and collided with Michael Hamilton as they both hurried for the door. Two more shots made Rebekah's ears ring.

She and Laramie got on the porch in time for Laramie to catch Steve. The young man had tripped on the top step and went sprawling across the porch.

Laramie grabbed him by the shoulders and righted him.

Steve gasped, "Jimmy's hurt, bad. Knifed. Lucky and the others are after the man who done it."

Before Steve finished, Doctor McKinnon was already rushing back into the house, and Rebekah knew he was getting her medical bag. She needed it, needed the grip Laramie had on her arm because she was already running down the stairs at full tilt, losing her balance on the last one.

He held her up and they ran together across the driveway and down the steps on the hill. At the bottom, swirling dust choked and blinded her. The ranch hands were riding out, firing at their target. They would've trampled Rebekah had it not been for Laramie's staying hand that kept her in place long enough for them to clear out.

The bunkhouse door hung open, lantern light shining from inside. Rebekah grabbed the door frame to swing inside, Laramie right behind her.

In the brightly lit interior, she rubbed grit from her eyes to see the round table where the boys played cards, the row of bunkbeds across from her, and the long eating table to her left.

That was where Stubby was bent over, not wholly unlike his usual work of serving meals. Only he was not. He was pressing both hands into a wound in Jimmy's gut as the young man lay stretched out on the table.

Rebekah ordered her feet to move. They somehow did, walking calmly, though rapidly, to the other side of the table as though this was simply the thousandth patient she'd treated in her medical career. But the sight of Jimmy's paling face nearly suffocated her.

He was unconscious, eyes closed, breathing shallow. Sweat caked the dirt on his forehead, his blonde hair matted in a muddy mess.

Judging from the amount of blood soaking his shirt and the pile of cloth Stubby pressed into the wound, she knew there wasn't much time.

Rebekah fumbled to unbutton her sleeves and roll them up as she said to Laramie and Steve behind her, "Get me hot water from the kitchen and Doctor McKinnon in here, quickly."

Steve ran out for the water as Doctor McKinnon and Michael Hamilton came inside.

Rebekah washed in the tepid water of the bowl near the door and turned back to Jimmy, catching Laramie's gaze. His steadiness calmed her even as he retrieved a rifle to stand guard at the open door.

She went back to the table. Doctor McKinnon set both their medical bags on it. Mercifully, Hamilton stayed out of the way.

Rebekah touched the back of Stubby's hand and he yielded. He didn't go far, only moving his hands enough for her to lift the makeshift bandage off the wound.

She held in a cry, then stiffened into action. She opened her medical bag and gathered what she needed, lining implements and bottles one by one next to Jimmy's shoulder. She refused to look at his face again, to see how fast life was leaving him.

Doctor McKinnon took Stubby's place as Steve came in, sloshing a pail of hot water onto the table by Jimmy's boots. He asked, "What else can I do, Doc?"

One word slipped through Rebekah's cold, stiff lips.

"Pray."

Laramie handed the rifle off to Steve and took up watch at the end of the table. Doctor McKinnon and Rebekah set to work, working in tandem.

They examined the wound and Doctor McKinnon took the lead in the operation. Rebekah allowed him, knowing he saw the tremble in her hands.

Within seconds, though, he paused and looked up at her. "He's lost too much blood. You know we must do it."

If it were possible, the chills spread deeper through Rebekah's body, from the roots of her hair to the tips of her toes. She couldn't move, couldn't breathe. The implication of Doctor McKinnon's words struck her wounded soul like a wet tree branch in fierce winds.

"No."

Somehow, Laramie was beside her, a warm hand on her arm. He tightened his grip enough to help her comprehend Doctor McKinnon's next words.

"If you don't give him a blood transfusion right now..." He didn't finish as he set to work on the wound, Stubby assisting him.

Laramie put his hand on Rebekah's other arm, turning her to face him. "The blood transfusion...will Jimmy die without it?"

Rebekah refused to meet his gaze, staring at her hands already stained with Jimmy's blood. She glanced over her shoulder at the precious boy who had become like a brother to her.

No.

A son.

She closed her eyes against the tears and Laramie squeezed her arms hard.

"Will he die without it?"

In a flash, Rebekah was three years in the past, back to the last patient she attempted an emergency blood transfusion on.

It failed.

Laramie's thumb dug into her forearm and she opened her eyes, swallowed, and whispered, "Yes."

Laramie released her and unbuttoned his right sleeve. He rolled it up.

"Then let's get at it."

Mechanically, Rebekah went to her bag and retrieved the double-ended blood transfusion apparatus, an instrument she had not used in three years.

While Stubby helped Doctor McKinnon repair damage done by the knife, Rebekah used a swab of alcohol to clean the skin above Laramie's vein and did the same on Jimmy's arm where Laramie had already rolled up the boy's sleeve.

Rebekah inserted the needle in Laramie's vein, then the other in Jimmy's, where so little blood was left.

*Please God.*

She began the pumps. "One...two...three..."

She heard Steve mutter roughly and it alarmed her. Was the attacker returning?

But when she looked up, the young man was standing calmly

in the doorway. Holding the rifle and looking into the darkness, his lips moved rapidly. Steve was praying.

"Nine... Ten... Eleven..."

Laramie flexed his fingers, doubtless feeling the tingle as blood transferred from his body to Jimmy's. There was nothing quite like giving blood to another, a part of one's self to save someone's life.

Or end it, if Jimmy's body rejected the blood.

Even now, researchers were making revolutionary discoveries about human blood types, but it wasn't advanced enough to use in practice. Certainly no help there on a ranch in rural Wyoming.

Rebekah felt her trembling start again and she couldn't remember the number she was on.

Laramie's voice cut through her fog. "Twenty-one...twenty-two..."

Rebekah allowed Laramie to finish the counts and she halted on the final one, breathing in the smell of alcohol and blood, sweat and dirt. She carefully removed the needle from Jimmy's arm, pressing a clean swab against the prick.

Laramie pulled the needle from his own arm and put an unwashed finger over the bleeding. She would have scolded him if Jimmy's face didn't still look so pale.

She pressed two fingers over the tiny hole in Jimmy's arm, refusing to look at the gaping one where Doctor McKinnon worked diligently. She leaned over Jimmy's shoulder and press her lips to his dirty forehead.

Stroking his hair with one hand, she whispered, "Now you fight, young man. Doc Beck's orders, and I'll see you have all the cinnamon rolls you can eat come morning."

Her voice cracked, and she swayed forward, resting partly across Jimmy. She cradled his head in her arms, her sobs coming as she remembered Freddy wasn't alive to make those cinnamon rolls.

From behind, Laramie held her.

She finally drew away and brushed aside her tears and every thought from her mind except what she could do as Doctor McKinnon finished the operation. He was prepared to sew the wound closed, sweat creating round spots on his shirt. Stubby wiped his boss's forehead.

Rebekah motioned for the threaded needle and Doctor McKinnon handed it over. She set about with her expert stitching. First in her class at medical school in wound care, no emotion was going to stop her and her uncle from giving Just Jimmy the absolute best care.

She had just finished and Doctor McKinnon began applying a clean bandage to the wound when the clomp of horse hooves set her heart to thundering again.

Laramie went to Steve at the door, and the young man nodded assurance. "It's our boys."

While Stubby cut the ruined shirt away from Jimmy, Lucky Saunders appeared in the doorway, casting a worried glance toward the table. Then he addressed Laramie.

"We chased the horses all the way to the foothills. The man was riding among them, but we couldn't find hide nor hair of him when we rounded up the horses. I sent two of the boys into town to get the marshal. I'll lead the men to keep looking, soon as our horses rest up."

Laramie shook his head. "Stable the horses and put out a triple guard. No man alone. We'll take up the hunt in the morning. Too dark to find anything now."

By the time Rebekah and Doctor McKinnon finished bandaging the wound and Stubby cleaned up from the operation, most of the McKinnon ranch hands had filtered into the bunkhouse, standing in a respectful half circle near the cots. Steve came to the foot of the table, hands in his back pockets.

"Want us to move Jimmy to a bed, ma'am? He can have mine. It's a lower bunk. Just tell us what we can do."

Rebekah shook her head as Doctor McKinnon answered. "We

won't move him yet, Steve. But you can do what Miss Becka said earlier...pray."

Lucky, his voice low and soft, asked, "Want me to ride for Preacher Wharton?"

Rebekah felt a sob rising in her chest. She took Jimmy's cold hand in hers, willing Laramie's blood to flow without hindrance. They would know soon.

Steve turned to Lucky. "We don't have to have a preacher to talk to the Almighty."

He tipped his head at the ranch hands, beckoning them toward the card table. The men gathered around it.

Laramie covered Jimmy with a blanket up to his chin, tucking it in close.

Rebekah held Jimmy's hand under the blanket, listening to the erratic rise and fall of cowboy voices. Sometimes the words were muttered, and then all would go quiet for a time. Then someone else began murmuring.

Once, gentle singing broke out, a range song like they used to soothe cattle. Several murmuring voices began then, prayers to the tune of the song as each man found his way to talk to God that dark, dark night.

# CHAPTER 16

The first streak of dawn had touched Jimmy's face, so drawn and aged, when Rebekah heard a dozen McKinnon cowboys mounting up outside the bunkhouse. They had filtered out in the predawn grayness, each coming by to check on Jimmy first and give her a pat on the shoulder.

Led by Steve, they were leaving with the dawn to hunt down the man who tried to take Jimmy's life. And might yet.

Laramie and Stubby, along with other hands, remained behind. Stubby was in his kitchen adjacent to the bunkhouse, making breakfast like it was a normal Sunday morning. But everyone knew it would be a long time before McKinnon Ranch was back to its old self, even after the killer was caught.

Rebekah was in a chair where she'd sat by Jimmy's side all night. The hard chair put a crick in her neck, and she rose to stretch to one side and then the other.

From the bunks near the table, Doctor McKinnon pushed himself upright with a grunt, his white shirt wrinkled and stained with dark blotches. He rubbed his eyes and blinked. How he was growing older, and more precious to Rebekah each day.

He got to his stockinged feet and came to Jimmy's other side. He used the back of his hand to feel the boy's forehead.

"How's our patient this morning?"

Rebekah never wanted to think of Jimmy as a patient. But she knew they both needed to hold themselves together and pull him through, Lord willing.

"He didn't reject the blood transfusion, at least not yet. The case studies I've read, though, and my own personal experience, it happens quickly."

Doctor McKinnon combed his fingers through Jimmy's loose hair. Rebekah had washed and dried it in the night. "He's a mighty fine young man. He'll pull through."

An incredible sense of relief went through Rebekah, and she collapsed into the chair, burying her face in her hands. But she didn't cry. She spent all her tears last night.

A warm hand rested on her shoulder, and she took it in her own before she realized it wasn't her uncle Robert.

Rebekah dropped her hand and looked up at Laramie.

"I've never known Doc McKinnon to be wrong," he said.

Across the table, Doctor McKinnon chuckled. "Maybe once or twice. But we know Jimmy, and I believe the good Lord has a lot more life for this young man to live on this earth."

He hesitated then met Laramie's eyes. Rebekah caught how Doctor McKinnon tipped his head toward the door. He wanted to speak to Laramie privately.

She stood. "What is it, Uncle Robert?"

Doctor McKinnon sighed. "Can't sneak a breath past you, can I, my dear? I need to speak to Laramie about what I discovered when treating the wound. He's going to see Marshal Thorp this morning."

Rebekah nodded for her uncle to go on. He carefully folded the blanket away from Jimmy to show the bandage right above his waist.

"See where the entry point is? Based on how the knife entered at an upward angle..." Doctor McKinnon used the flat of his hand to illustrate "...the man was either squatting low and sprang upward, or..."

Doctor McKinnon folded the blanket back up to Jimmy's chin and met Rebekah's eyes. "Or it could've been a man with no legs."

Rebekah stared at him, trying to connect the pieces he had mulled over in the night. She blinked, fatigue clouding her mind.

Laramie slowly ticked off points by counting them on his fingers. "One; the sideshow ticket someone sent Becka with the bloody thumb print over the ape man's face. Two; the knife used on...Freddy. Was it the same size as this one?"

Doctor McKinnon nodded. "I took a look at Freddy's wound. It was a wide knife, like a Bowie knife. Same dimensions and depth as Jimmy's, from what I could tell."

Rebekah fought to make a connection to that point. "Hamilton said a large knife was used on Will Flit, the former sideshow manager, and we know the same about Senator Harris."

Laramie touched a third finger, then his pinky. "Fourth; the blue roan Jimmy saw the legless man riding by the Little Medicine Bow River." Now his thumb. "Five; the low angle of the wound."

Rebekah covered her mouth, trying to make sense of the conversation. She lowered her fingers to her chin. "Do you think the so-called ape man is behind all of this? Including Senator Harris?"

Laramie turned to her. "Will you go to town with me, Becka? Talk to the marshal and tell him what you know?"

Like her heart, Rebekah felt herself pulled in two. She didn't want to leave Jimmy, but they had to discover the madman who was picking off those she loved, one by one.

"I will go with you."

# CHAPTER 17

When Rebekah, Laramie, and Marshal Thorp arrived at the circus camp, nearly all the tents were down. The crew people loading canvases into the wagons gave the trio sharp looks.

The night before, the marshal cleared them to leave town, and they appeared in a hurry. But there were a few tents still up and Marshal Thorp guided them to a solid black one. The ape man's tent.

Marshal Thorp ducked through the open door, Laramie and Rebekah behind him. Three trunks sat near a tri-fold partition on one side, and the plump sideshow manager was on the other side, folding a cot. He dropped it with a thud. "I thought you people were going to leave us alone."

The marshal skipped answering the question to ask his own. "Where's the legless man? And on that note, what is his real name?"

"You got no business here, Marshal, and unless you got a search warrant, you get on out of here."

In a smooth motion, Marshal Thorp withdrew a paper from his shirt pocket. "Just so happens the judge is up and about this

Sunday morning. We're going to search this tent, so you just unlock those trunks."

The plump man crossed his arms. "I don't do nothing unless the circus manager or ringmaster tells me to."

Laramie swept his left arm toward Rebekah and Marshal Thorp, moving them to the side while he drew and cocked his six-gun. Before anyone could say a word, Laramie shot the lock off the largest trunk. The plump man jumped and ran out the door.

Marshal Thorp opened the trunk and began lifting out stacks of costuming, checking between each item. Ears ringing from the gunshot, Rebekah knelt and lifted out a box marked *make-up* to search it. From the corner of her eye, she saw the gunshot had drawn attention. A crowd of circus people gathered outside the tent door.

Laramie reached between Marshal Thorp and Rebekah to heft out a pile of unfolded clothes. As soon as his shadow moved and light fell inside the trunk, Rebekah gasped. Laying in the bottom was a large Bowie knife.

Marshal Thorp picked it up and held it in the full light. Rebekah reached one hand out. "May I?"

He handed it over and Rebekah felt the heaviness of the bone handle and long blade. She turned it carefully and held it close to her eyes. Flecks of dried blood were stuck between the blade and the handle.

She swallowed and handed the knife to Laramie, indicating what she found, while Marshal Thorp snagged one last thing from the bottom of the trunk. A stack of stationery.

He fanned the blank pages. "Same stationery as the note we found by Freddy."

A thud sounded behind Rebekah. Laramie dropped the knife to draw and aim his gun over her head.

On her knees beside the trunk, Rebekah swiveled to find herself face-to-face with the ape man.

He'd dragged himself from behind the partition and was

hunched forward on his fists, staring straight at her. He was dressed in a shirt and string tie, the legs on his trousers pinned behind him. The fake beard he wore for the show was gone and his hair was combed back.

Without the grungy make-up, Rebekah finally recognized him. "Toby Blackthorn."

The man didn't blink, didn't seem surprised to be face-to-face with the doctor who had amputated his legs.

Laramie kept his gun on the man. "You know him, Becka?"

Rebekah slowly nodded. "He was in a logging accident in Nevada a few years ago. The doctor at the hospital where Mr. Blackthorn was taken confirmed I did the right thing. But still..." She never broke her gaze away from Toby Blackthorn. She added quietly, "I'm so sorry."

Marshal Thorp held up the stationery and Bowie knife. "Are these yours, Mr. Blackthorn?"

Toby Blackthorn nodded.

"Then you are under arrest for the murder of Freddy Goodman. When we get this untangled, we might have a few more charges to add. "

Laramie used his free hand to help Rebekah up, pulling her securely away from the man who never took his eyes off her. Laramie asked Toby Blackthorn, "Did you have any accomplices?"

The man shook his head, his eyes still on Rebekah. She could sense anger and bitterness buried beneath the layers of his gaze. But somehow, she didn't feel it was directed solely at her.

# CHAPTER 18

Rebekah and Laramie remained in town to wait for Marshal Thorp to question Toby Blackthorn. He did it in the cells while Rebekah and Laramie waited in his office, writing out their full testimonies.

It didn't take long before the marshal emerged, closing the door leading to the cells behind him with a heavy sigh. "Couldn't get a word out of him. Not even if he wanted me to fetch a lawyer. I can see why he didn't have friends from the circus come to his defense."

Rebekah had thought that odd as well. When they departed with Toby Blackthorn under arrest, the crowd outside the man's tent made way for them without objection. They didn't seem glad to see him go. They looked fearful.

Marshal Thorp went to his desk and scanned the two pages Laramie and Rebekah had written with all the information they could think of. There was still a big missing piece that none of them could pin down.

Before they could talk about what it was, Michael Hamilton strolled through the open door. In all the trauma the night before, Rebekah had forgotten about him.

"Marshal Thorp, the killer has been arrested!" Hamilton declared.

Rebekah came to her feet and Hamilton swirled, seeing her and Laramie.

"Oh! Doc Beck. Most appropriate that you're here. Stanley Cook, Senator Harris's assistant, has been arrested for his murder."

Marshal Thorp dropped the papers on his desk and put his hands on his hips. "What a coincidence. We just arrested the murderer of Freddy, and likely the man who stabbed young Jimmy."

Hamilton's eyebrows furrowed and he rubbed his chin then tapped it with his finger. "I think we have it now, Marshal. I took the late-night train into Cheyenne and pounded on Marshal Phillips' door early this morning. We confronted Stanley Cook and it didn't take much to break him. Said a man paid him to do the dirty deed, though Cook had his own grudge against Harris. Seems Harris was preventing Cook from marrying his daughter and sent her off to school where she is now engaged. Mild Stanley didn't take it lightly."

Laramie crossed his arms. Rebekah knew he had no love for Michael Hamilton, even after this revelation.

But he was willing to give an inch. "What does he know about the man who paid him?"

"Never saw him. Cook received an anonymous note to meet him in a warehouse where the man kept talking to him but would never show himself. Said he had a deep, quiet voice, and it scared Cook into the deal as much as it nearly scared him out of it. Cook believed he could get the girl in the end, if her father were out of the way."

While Hamilton wrapped up the story, Rebekah wondered what Toby Blackthorn's voice sounded like. He hadn't spoken since they encountered him.

He'd been in such pain prior to the amputation, all she heard were high pitched screams, him begging her to save his legs. What was a man in the west without his legs?

The image of the ape man illustration with its bloody thumbprint over Toby Blackthorn's face came vividly to Rebekah's mind. She now knew what she'd done to make the killer so vengeful.

It was horrible to think about it all, so she directed her attention to the newspaperman. "Thank you for your assistance in the case, Mr. Hamilton. It's a relief to know it's finally over."

Hamilton removed his derby hat and swept it toward the door. "May I speak with you a moment, Miss Rebekah?" To Laramie, he added cheerfully, "Don't worry, I'll bring her right back."

Rebekah stepped onto the porch of the jail with Michael Hamilton while Laramie and Marshal Thorp conversed. She noticed Laramie positioned himself to see out the large picture windows, keeping an eye on her even though the danger was finally passed.

She turned to the intrepid newspaper reporter. "What is on your mind, Mr. Hamilton?"

Hamilton looked more hesitant than she'd seen him since they met. More serious, too, though not as serious as most men. He drew in a deep breath as though filling himself with enough air to present a speech without pausing.

"Miss Rebekah, I have a confession of my own. I'm not only a reporter. You see, in my former days before switching professions to the newspaper business, I was with the Pinkerton Detective Agency."

Rebekah took a step back, eyebrows raised. "No wonder you do so well with investigating."

"A little too well."

She cocked her head, prompting him to go on. He did, avoiding her gaze. "I had a fine reputation as an agent, even got myself a measure of fame. It always found me in the oddest places. Most recently, that odd place was in Cheyenne some months back, right after I released my first article about you. A man came to me and, well, he gave me a different side to your story that I found hard to believe. But given he was a reputable man, my investigative instincts got the better of me; and I flat out needed the money at the time, so I agreed to his proposal. The man was Indian Agent Roger Graham."

Rebekah clenched her hand into a fist and pressed it against her stomach. "And what was that proposal, Mr. Hamilton?"

He sighed. "To investigate you, Doc Beck. He knew you were still practicing medicine and making plans to return to the Omaha Indian Reservation. Though he is no longer an agent there, he adamantly opposes you practicing medicine anywhere."

Rebekah pressed her fist harder, and Hamilton hurried on. "I never took a side, Miss Rebekah. Truly. But that is why I've been around more. Yet I can tell you as a skilled investigator, which I've now proven, I found no reason for you to not return to the Omaha Indian Reservation, and by thunder, I'll do everything I can to support it!"

Rebekah uncurled her fist and let her hand dropped to her side, suddenly spent.

"Thank you, Mr. Hamilton."

His eyes brightened and he plopped his derby hat back on his head. "Miss Rebekah, I'm running a distant third to Laramie Jones and your first love, the Omaha people, and will never catch up. But would you do me the honor of taking supper in town with me?"

Rebekah glanced inside the jail again and met Laramie's gaze. To Hamilton, she said, "I'm sorry, Michael, but I need to return to the ranch now. That is my home, and we have healing to do."

Michael Hamilton gave a stout nod. "You calling me Michael is honor enough. I'm sure we'll see one another down the road, Doc Beck. You always make for a good story."

With a mile left to home, Laramie and Rebekah slowed from a lope to give the horses and themselves a breather. They weren't making a mad dash back to the ranch like after Laramie's ambush, but after all the news at the marshal's office, they felt the urgency to get home. They had to see about Jimmy.

It would take that last mile to cool the horses in the hot Wyoming sun. Rebekah wanted to push all the way to the end, but thinking of Jimmy's love for horses helped her rein in.

But she couldn't rein her tongue in, and she turned her face toward the heavens.

"Why!"

She choked and brought her voice down. "Why, Lee? Why did men die because of me?"

Her voice caught on tears and she was too exhausted to truly show anger. She just wanted an answer.

Laramie reached across the distance between the horses and touched her forearm. "There's evil in this world I don't think we were meant to understand, Becka. But we were meant to fight it."

They rode in silence, Rebekah taking the words in. She did fight it. She was meant to.

Her heart lifted at the sight of the final gate that stood on the hill before the road dipped into the valley with the McKinnon ranch house and bunkhouse nestled in. It would be in sight in moments.

Laramie shifted in his saddle so that he faced her. "Now that it's over, I reckon you'll get back to figuring out how to return to the reservation. But before you do, Becka, we need to have a nice long talk, the one you haven't wanted to."

Rebekah stiffened and Laramie sighed. "We've avoided this for most of three years, but..."

His gaze drifted to what had Rebekah's attention. They had just topped the rise and into view of the McKinnon Ranch house sitting high with the bunkhouse, barn, and corrals below it.

Several ranch hands were gathered around the open doorway to the bunkhouse.

Laramie and Rebekah urged the horses to a full gallop. In the barnyard, Rebekah came to such a sudden stop, it nearly unseated her. Laramie was off his horse and helping her down before she regained her balance.

He swung her to the ground and she gripped his forearms, hard, fear pulsing through her. He nodded, somehow transferring a bit of his sturdy strength to her.

She swallowed and turned to press through the ranch hands who made way for her. Steve was leaned back against the door jam, the color gone from his face. He met her eyes and his lips moved, but no words came out.

In a fog, Rebekah stepped across the threshold and stared at the table. It was empty.

# CHAPTER 19

Rebekah couldn't move, couldn't breathe as she stared at the bloodstained table where she last saw Jimmy. Her knees buckled and Steve caught her from behind.

"Miss Becka, it's..."

"Doc Beck!"

The yelp sent a surge of energy through Rebekah. She pushed the door all the way open to reveal the bunks at the far-right side. Laying on a bottom one, being pinned down by Doctor McKinnon, was a very alive Jimmy!

Rebekah let out a cry and rushed forward as her young friend flailed one arm at her.

"Miss Rebekah! No one will tell me, did I miss it? I don't wanna miss it."

Rebekah could see his eyes were clear, no fever. But he was straining hard to get out of bed. Doctor McKinnon held a firm hand against Jimmy's bandaged wound, shaking his head.

"He must've heard you coming, because he woke up suddenly, hollering for you and asking if he missed it. Scared all of the boys right out of the room."

Rebekah knelt by the cot and held Jimmy's face between her

hands, savoring the warmth of his flesh that had been so cold. Laramie's blood must have been very right for Jimmy.

"What is it, Jimmy? What are you worried you missed?"

"My baptism, Miss Rebekah. Got to get it done before winter."

Rebekah sucked in a breath, and it came out in a mixture of laughter and tears.

Jimmy's eyes clouded over. "You all right, ma'am? Someone hurt you while I was out?"

Rebekah shook her head and pulled Jimmy into a tight hug, stroking the back of his head. He relaxed in her embrace, cocking his head to rest on hers.

He whispered, "It's all right, Miss Rebekah. I'm all right."

Indeed, he was. Laramie's blood had saved his life and Christ's blood saved his soul. Jimmy would be able to show the world both of those lives with his baptism soon.

# CHAPTER 20

The day of Freddy's funeral was one of the hardest of Rebekah's life. She awoke Monday morning and broke down at the smell of cinnamon rolls wafting through the house.

When she went downstairs and found Stubby in the kitchen, pulling out another dozen rolls, she honored him with taking the first bite and was shocked by the vibrant flavor that marked Freddy's cinnamon rolls.

Stubby confessed that he'd always known Freddy's secret ingredient, but never wanted to take away his brother's pride in it.

After the morning's funeral service at the church, everyone was content to get back to work. Laramie Jones had a list of supplies to order in town, and the rest of the hands returned to the bunkhouse long enough to change clothes to catch up on all the work they'd fallen behind on.

Rebekah had contemplated visiting Toby Blackthorn at the jail, but she didn't have the strength to confront him after the funeral. She heard Stubby did as he remained in town with a few other hands while Doctor McKinnon and Rebekah headed home.

As soon as the buggy stopped in front of the house,

Rebekah was off, up the stairs, and to the second floor. They had moved Jimmy from the bunkhouse to where Rebekah could keep a close watch on him in the guest room across from her room.

He was grieved not to attend Freddy's funeral, but Rebekah and Doctor McKinnon concurred he should remain in bed to recover from the wound he shouldn't have survived. If Rebekah hadn't believed in miracles before, she did now.

She tapped on the open door as she entered his room, surprised to see she wasn't the only visitor.

Jimmy was propped up slightly in bed, surrounded by the Palmer triplets who were piled in the king-sized bed around him, Valor the dog laying across his legs.

Rebekah smiled. "Well, I see you aren't lacking good company, Jimmy. Did you ring the silver bell I gave you and summon the children from town?"

Wayne, who was up on his knees beside Jimmy, solemnly shook his head. "No, ma'am. We come here on our own. We wanted to see that Just Jimmy was all right, and to tell him he ain't got to worry about Uncle Rufus no more, if he was ever worried about him."

Rebekah removed pins from her hat and laid it on the low dresser. "What do you mean?"

"A tramp that came from the foothills of the Medicine Bow Mountains told us that Uncle Rufus fell off a cliff and got hurt bad. We snuck up there to see him, but we were scared he'd die in front of us. We come straight here."

Rebekah leaned over Roy, who was snuggled on Jimmy's good side, and felt Jimmy's forehead. It was cool to the touch and his eyes were still clear, but troubled.

Jimmy swallowed. "I know that Rufus is a mean man, ma'am. But...no one should die alone, should they?"

She lowered into a chair next to the bed. "No, Jimmy, I suppose they shouldn't." She looked to the twins. "I'll see that someone looks after your uncle, but you children should get back to town. The Robinsons will be worried."

Wayne slipped off the bed while Willie and Roy gave Rebekah hugs before the triplets left the room, Valor bounding after them.

While Rebekah watched them disappear, Jimmy said, "Miss Rebekah, I know the man who stabbed me. But I don't know *who* it was, and it's bothering me something fierce."

She turned to look at him, head cocked. Did he forget she told him Toby Blackthorn had been arrested? Jimmy did know the man, sort of. He'd seen him in the sideshow and on posters.

She patted his hand. "It's all right, Jimmy. It's over now."

# CHAPTER 21

If Laramie Jones or Doctor McKinnon knew where Rebekah was headed, they wouldn't believe it.

She scarcely believed it herself as she urged her horse up the steep trail in the foothills of the Medicine Bow Mountains. Just a few days before, no one would let her out of their sight.

Now she was completely alone and it was a relief. She spent most of the previous three years of her life traveling alone in the west. Being at the ranch under guard was smothering. The cool air of the foothills, the lodgepole pines, and stunning rock formations refreshed her soul. Even at that, though, she was not being entirely selfish in her ride.

Like Jimmy said, no one should die alone.

She'd heard rumors in town of where Rufus Palmer was holed up, prospecting in gold-less creeks in the foothills and likely living in one of the unused line cabins on the McKinnon Ranch.

Rebekah didn't want to ask any of the ranch hands nor her exhausted uncle Robert to make the ride out. She left a note in the parlor where he would find it easily. Everyone had lost enough time and she'd cost enough production on McKinnon Ranch without pulling anyone away. She was simply on another medical mission, and that felt right.

The cabin came into sight and Rebekah slowed her horse. The cabin did look abandoned except for the mule in a rope corral near it.

As Rebekah entered the yard, she called, "Hello the house!"

If Rufus was capable of shooting off the shotgun he liked to threaten people with, she wanted it to go off before she was close.

There was no answer from the house, gunshot or otherwise. Rebekah urged her horse close to the hitching rail by the front porch and dismounted, unhooking her medical bag from the saddle. She stepped onto the porch and stood to the side of the door as she wrapped on it firmly. "Mr. Palmer? It's Doctor LaRoche. I've come to help."

A moan sounded inside and Rebekah took that as an invitation to enter.

She pushed the door open, allowing sunlight into the room from it and the windows on each side of it. After her eyes adjusted to the dimmer interior, she saw it was outfitted like a standard line cabin.

A single table took up the center with two chairs, a cabinet and stove were crammed along another wall, and a window on the back wall could let in a breeze from the north in summers. A cot was situated on the right wall, and laid out on that cot, letting loose another moan, was Rufus Palmer.

Bag in hand, Rebekah stepped around the debris-littered floor where Rufus had flung his boots, gold pans, and sacks in a hapless manner. She reached the cot and carefully lifted one of Rufus' eyelids. The man groaned and Rebekah had that sickening knowledge that came with her years of experience. Barring a miracle, he wasn't going to make it.

But still, she pulled a chair close and proceeded with her examination. Minutes later, she took hold of his rough, scarred hand.

"Mr. Palmer, your injuries are severe. I'm going to give you something for the pain, but there is nothing I can do for you here. We can attempt to transfer you to the hospital in Cheyenne, but I fear you would not be able to endure the long trip. Do you understand?"

Rufus growled and jerked his hand away. "Git out and leave me alone, woman."

"I am a doctor and obligated to render aid to anyone who needs it, Mr. Palmer. Unless you physically throw me out, I am going to stay and help you any way I can."

Rufus tried to turn away from her, but his broken body caused him to scream in pain.

Rebekah drew a needle of laudanum and administered it. Rufus calmed, and she knew the only thing left to do was pray for him. And so she did.

❧

RUFUS WAS UNCONSCIOUS, sweating, and his breathing grew shallower by the minute. He was slipping away, just as the day was.

Rebekah was acutely aware of the sun's passage through the sky as it made its way to sunset. But she couldn't leave Rufus to die alone, no matter his meanness. There was always a chance for repentance and she would remain to give him that chance. If he cried out for mercy in his last moments, she wanted to tell him it could be granted to him.

But he had not cried out and Rebekah lit the lamp by the cot and went to close the cabin door against the evening chill. She should start a fire in the cookstove and make coffee. It could be a long night, though in her professional opinion, it wouldn't be.

As she shut the door, her horse let out a whinny and Rufus' mule answered.

Jolted, Rebekah pushed the door closed a little too hard. She took a deep breath. Even though the killer, or killers when she included Stanley Cook, had been arrested, it could take time for her to feel fully composed.

But then, neither Toby Blackthorn nor Stanley Cook had been proven guilty yet. Was there a chance there were more accomplices?

Before Rebekah could think that through, the window to her right broke with a loud crash, a rock striking the cold stove.

She gasped and ran for her medical bag. After dumping it out at the end of the cot, she struggled with the false bottom. In the quiet consumed only by her breathing, she realized two things: Rufus had passed. But she was not alone.

As her hand gripped the pepperbox, which held four cartridges, she heard distant laughter coming through the broken window. Rebekah bent over the lamp by the cot and blew it out. She turned to look out the broken window, seeing where shadows were beginning to dance in the dusky light.

Then a deep, cool voice called out. "Doctor Rebekah LaRoche! Your reputation precedes you. To be fair, I will allow my reputation to precede me."

Rebekah was sure she'd never heard the man's voice before, but it sent a shiver of terror through her. She pressed her back against the side wall of the cabin to where she could see both front windows, the door, and the back window.

The voice came again, this time from the east side and Rebekah swung her pistol in that direction, aiming at the wall.

"It's only fair you know who I am before I kill you. I am Calvin Blackthorn, lately of the Donovan Brothers Circus. But before that—indeed, long, long before that, I was the younger brother of the finest man who ever lived—Toby Blackthorn. The man you butchered."

Rebekah held her breath, trying to keep up with his stream of words and the direction they were coming from. There was a state of silence and her eyes stared at the broken window again. But the voice came from the opposite direction.

"I don't believe you did everything you could for my brother like you claimed. Instead, you resigned him to a life as a sideshow freak. Everyone enjoyed laughing at him, especially his former manager, Will Flit. Flit laughed at him up to the moment I killed him. That Laramie Jones and the boy were lucky. I'm not usually that clumsy."

Rebekah shifted down the wall, still trying to follow the voice and stay opposite of it.

When the silence stretched long, Rebekah inched forward, thinking to use the table as a shield between her and Calvin Blackthorn. But the next time the voice came it was not in front of her. It was near the wall behind her.

"Your uncle was next, if you hadn't had my brother arrested."

The closeness of his voice sent Rebekah skittering forward. She tripped on one of Rufus' boots and hit her knee on the floor. She heard a chuckle and aimed her pepperbox at the wall. She fired where she judged the man to be.

Silence again.

Rebekah scooted away from the table and to the back wall. She stilled, straining to hear. She didn't realize how close she was to the back window until the glass in it shattered.

Gasping, she swung her pistol that direction as an arm darted inside. She fired at the arm, then through the wall. The arm retracted with a screeching sound.

She wanted to fire again, lower where she imagined the man doubled over from his wounds, if she managed to hit him with both bullets. But she only had one left.

Silence again, then footsteps scraped slow and long across the front porch. Rebekah took a quick breath, her eyes watering from gun smoke, and fear. She saw the doorknob turning.

The door made a click, and she took aim. With a mighty

surge, the door swung inward. Rebekah squeezed the trigger on her last round and the bullet flew through the empty doorway.

There was a chuckle as Calvin Blackthorn swung around to lean against the door jam.

In the dusky light, Rebekah could see blood soaking his black ringmaster coat and red vest. There was a chance she'd hit the brachial artery in his arm.

He swung his top hat off to bow his tall, lean frame at her.

"Ladies and gentlemen, I give you the infamous Doc Beck!"

Rebekah grabbed one of the chairs, swung it up and over her shoulder, the only weapon she had. Calvin Blackthorn straightened off the door jam and reached beneath his coat to draw out a long Bowie knife.

"We can make this quick and easy, Doc, or slow and hard like you did for my brother."

He took a step inside, eyes widening as he fought to take a second step.

Then Calvin Blackthorn tipped forward and landed facedown with a thud.

The silence of the moment overwhelmed Rebekah.

Eyes still trained on the doorway, she saw a rider entering the clearing of the yard.

Laramie Jones. Lee.

Rebekah dropped the chair and it clattered to the floor louder than any gunshot. Blackness overtook her vision and the next thing she knew, Lee was holding her where she had collapsed into his arms.

She didn't know what had happened. She only knew she was always safe with him.

# CHAPTER 22

The air was nippy on the banks of Omaha Lake, but no one seemed to mind. Least of all Rebekah as she observed the gathering ranch hands there to witness Jimmy's baptism on the edge of the lake trimmed with pines of bright green.

His wound was healed well enough for him to enter the lake water. Rebekah didn't clear him until yesterday and he immediately wanted to get baptized the next day, along with anyone else who wanted.

Now that the threat was truly over with Calvin Blackthorn's death, everyone was ready for a rebirth.

On the ride home from the foothills, Laramie told Rebekah what transpired while she was sitting at the bedside of Rufus Palmer.

Toby Blackthorn had sent for the ringmaster to visit him in jail. When he learned the ringmaster was not among the crew pitching tents for another overnight stay, he went into a frenzy. Laramie was still in town and Marshal Thorp called on him as a witness while Toby confessed everything.

The blue roan, the knife, and stationery were his brother's.

Toby knew Calvin hid the weapon in the trunk because he thought it was the last place anyone would look, that no one would suspect a legless man capable of anything beyond a circus act.

Toby said his brother Calvin never accepted the loss of Toby's legs. He swore revenge on the doctor who amputated them. But Toby hadn't thought he was serious and went on with his life, which led him to the circus sideshow for the past two years.

Calvin wouldn't let it go and when he read the article about Doc Beck, he devised a scheme to exact revenge. He set out to not only ruin her dream of returning to the Omaha Indian Reservation, but to cause Rebekah deep pain before he targeted her own life.

In almost every sense, Calvin Blackthorn had been successful.

But in the end, it was he who lost his life and Rebekah given the chance to live hers anew. Whether that was on the Omaha Indian Reservation or, as Laramie wanted to talk about—settling forever in Wyoming.

Toby Blackthorn was beginning his life anew as well. He quit the sideshow and took a train to St. Louis, Missouri, to accept a job offer as a warehouse clerk from an old friend. The conjoined twins, Bernard and Arnold, went with him to take a try at city life.

People from church began to arrive at the lake, including the Robinsons and Palmer triplets. Jimmy had held them close in the king-sized bed while they cried some over the loss of their uncle. Then Wayne astonished him by asking if, instead of Mr. Jimmy or Just Jimmy, they could call him Uncle Jimmy.

He'd looked to Rebekah for permission, and she thought it was a fine idea.

It appeared everyone who was coming to the baptism—a sizable crowd with neighboring ranchers like the Butlers and Wallaces and the '76 outfit—was there. Jimmy had made many friends in Wyoming.

Rebekah observed the faces of the McKinnon Ranch crew that were touched with sadness, most especially over Freddy's death. Stubby was his usual stiff, cantankerous self, but something had broken inside him. Rebekah knew he would never be the same. None of them would.

Despite the joyous setting, a surge of anger spread through her. Calvin Blackthorn had no right to inflict so much damage on innocent people. Yet he had, and Rebekah knew she must forgive him. But must she right at that moment?

She'd forgiven so many in recent months, yet she knew putting it off would not make it easier. That had been the case with Indian Agent Roger Graham and what he'd done to separate her from her people; her home.

Then the anger was dislodged with a jolt of realization. She had yet to forgive Agent Graham. She did not know which man was harder to forgive in that moment.

The time had come, signaled by Pastor Wharton leading the way into the lake. Laramie Jones followed. Jimmy had asked Laramie to stand with him for the baptism.

Jimmy was next, supported by Steve, who helped him to the bank. Laramie started to take Jimmy, but Steve shook his head. He cast a glance over his shoulder at his fellow ranch hands.

Steve cleared his throat and said loud enough for all to hear, "I reckon I might as well get dunked, too, since I'm going to be more than a Sunday-only, God-fearing cowboy."

Rebekah didn't miss the joy that exploded on Jimmy's face as he grinned at his friend, arm hooked around his shoulder. Steve shrugged sheepishly and mostly dragged Jimmy into the water.

Pastor Wharton stood with his arms spread wide, his face solemn in the sunshine. "Steve Bowers has the right idea. Baptism is open to anyone who makes a public declaration of their faith in Jesus Christ as the son of God. Anyone who desires to make that proclamation and be baptized here today, may."

Pastor Wharton proceeded to ask Jimmy for that proclamation, then he and Laramie gently lowered Jimmy back, immersing him in the lake water.

Jimmy came up sputtering and spitting as he laughed and flung water droplets from his hair. Laramie gripped him in a hug, then reached to shake Steve's hand. Rebekah was sure it was more than lake water on Laramie's face.

Tears spilled from her eyes as well, especially when, moments after Steve was baptized, Lucky Saunders moved to the bank. He sniffed and rubbed one finger under his nose. He started to look back at the other hands, but then squared himself with the pastor and gave a resolute nod.

Pastor Wharton beckoned him forward. If Lucky had looked back, he would see Stubby following him, along with five other McKinnon ranch hands.

They'd all done a lot of trying to find their way to talk to God that dark night when Jimmy was nearly killed. But they truly found it that Sunday afternoon as cowhand after cowhand was baptized.

None of them wanted to leave the waist-high water after their dunk, opting to stay close and share grins and handshakes with one another, Laramie, and Jimmy.

Rebekah was worried about Jimmy staying in the cold water too long, but she'd never seen him quite so happy.

Pastor Wharton called, "Is there anyone else ready to make their public proclamation?"

Jimmy met Rebekah's eyes and his grin faded. She knew the shadows on her own face showed even in the Wyoming sun. And he knew why.

He told her something true awhile back, and it rang in her heart now. *Forgiveness is simple. It's just not easy.*

Rebekah blinked the tears from her eyes enough to see where she stepped through the pine needles to the water's edge.

Jimmy's eyes grew rounder and Steve turned toward her, along with Laramie Jones.

She hesitated, thinking of the Sunday best dress she wore. Then she squatted and unlaced her boots, slipping them off along with her stockings to feel the earth on her bare feet.

A thrill went through her, a connection with the land and the Creator who made all. It was time.

She took a step into the water, sinking into the mud that covered her toes and reminded her that she was connected to creation no matter where in the world she was.

She took another step forward, and another, until Laramie reached out his hand to steady her next to Pastor Wharton. She drew in a deep breath, chilled from the cold water and the movement in her soul.

"Pastor, it is my desire to make a public declaration as a woman who believes that Jesus Christ is the Son of God, my Savior who gives me the power to forgive."

She barely heard the words that Pastor Wharton spoke over her. She closed her eyes and felt herself tipping back, all the hurt and pain and grief and scars of her life pressing her down.

The water covered her, then she was raised up in the sunshine and, like a flash of lightning, truth lit up her heart.

No one made it through life unscathed. But they could be reborn and receive the new life that awaited them each day.

Rebekah laughed, the sound ringing loud in her ears as she brushed wet hair from her face. Jimmy threw his arms around her and she hugged him tight.

What a family God had blessed her with in this season of life.

But when Rebekah opened her eyes, she saw something that utterly took her breath away.

A man was standing on the bank. A man she had known from the moment of birth.

She blinked, wondering if he would disappear, but he didn't.

The man was her brother. Amos LaRoche.

Jimmy, his back to the bank, pointed at the sky with his chin. "Look, Miss Rebekah."

She turned her face upward, toward the shafts of light filtering through the golden-white clouds.

Jimmy rested his head on her shoulder, worn out. He whispered, "A little light sure creates a lot of beauty, don't it?"

There were so many questions surrounding the next season of Rebekah's life, but they could wait another moment for answers.

Rebekah rested her head on top of Jimmy's, this brilliant light in her life.

"Yes, Just Jimmy. It certainly does."

◈

Dearest reader,

Thank you for reading *Ape Man (Doc Beck Westerns Book 8)*. I truly hope it entertained and delighted you!

If you fell in love with the main characters, Rebekah, aka "Doc Beck," and Jimmy, you'll be excited to know there are more books to come! Books 9-12 are slated to release in 2022.

Meanwhile, I'd be thrilled if you took a moment to write your thoughts in the form of a review for *Ape Man* and post it on your favorite retail outlet and Goodreads. You'll help other readers find this series.

To discover more of my books, free short stories, and to generally stay in touch with me, I invite you to join my VIP reader newsletter. You'll receive a free copy of *The Executions*, book one in my *Choctaw Tribune* Historical Fiction series. Please join me through: bit.ly/ChoctawTribune.

Speaking of history, the character of Doc Beck was inspired by Dr. Susan La Flesche (Omaha), who is hailed as the first American Indian to earn a medical degree. In continued research, my mother found Dr. Isabel Cobb (Cherokee), the first woman physician in Indian Territory, in very nearly the same years as Dr. La Flesche.

Lastly, if you're not familiar with my heritage books based on my Choctaw history and culture, you can check them out on www.SarahElisabethWrites.com.

Questions? Send them my way: me@sarahelisabethwrites.com

—Sarah Elisabeth Sawyer
Historical Fiction and Western author
Tribal member of the Choctaw Nation of Oklahoma

men willing to die—and kill—for a wild piece of land just as dangerous as any bullet?

***Canyon War* is available on multiple retailer sites.**

♦♦♦

*MISSION BANDITS (DOC BECK WESTERNS BOOK 2)*

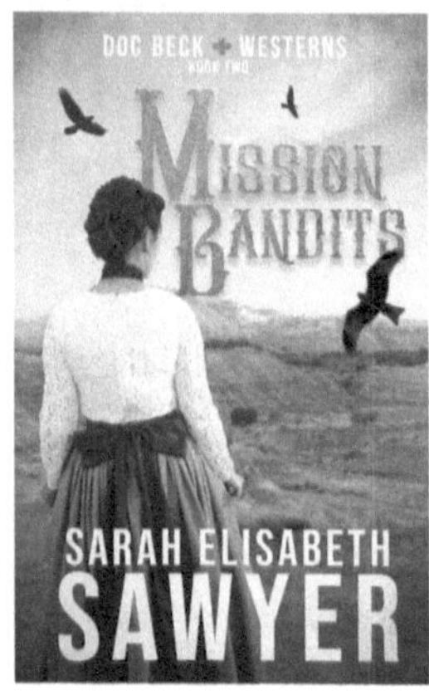


The Mexican army, a town marshal, and the Sancho Guerra gang are facing off when Doctor Rebekah LaRoche and her new friend, Jimmy, arrive in Zapata, New Mexico Territory. The bandits are holding hostages at Hope Academy, a school for girls located in an old mission outside of town, and Rebekah feels compelled to act—she was sent to the school to modernize the infirmary, not see the innocent occupants murdered.

The notorious and charismatic bandit, Sancho Guerra, led his band of men on a pillaging spree from Mexico to the mission and has proven his indifference to killing, prepared for any tricks the army or the Zapata town marshal throw at him.

But he isn't prepared for Rebekah, and now the Mexican army colonel wants her to do something terrifying—enter the mission and help with the capture of the deadliest men in the territory.

***Mission Bandits* is available on multiple retailer sites.**

*DESERT CAPTIVE (DOC BECK WESTERNS BOOK 4)*

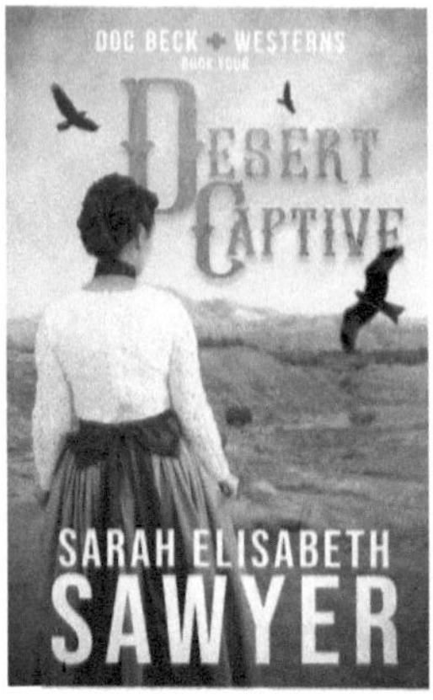

*If thou knewest the gift of God...thou wouldest have asked of him, and he would have given thee living water...*

There comes a time when one questions every decision they've made in life. That moment is here for Doctor Rebekah LaRoche when she is taken captive by her nemesis, the bandit Sancho Guerra, and spirited across the desert to a hidden village in Mexico.

With no hope of rescue, Rebekah must earn a place among the families of bandits as a medical doctor until she can devise a way to reach the top of the road leading out of the valley—without being shot by the three sets of guards.

Little does Rebekah know that her long-time friend, Laramie Jones, is on his way to attempt a hopeless rescue. If she knew his plans, she'd beg him to stay away: no one has ever penetrated the bandits' valley and lived to tell about it.

With factions closing in all around her, time is ticking down toward an explosive conclusion, and Rebekah will have to draw on her greatest strength yet to survive.

***Desert Captive* is available on multiple retailer sites.**

◆◆◆

*RANCH FEUD (DOC BECK WESTERNS BOOK 5)*

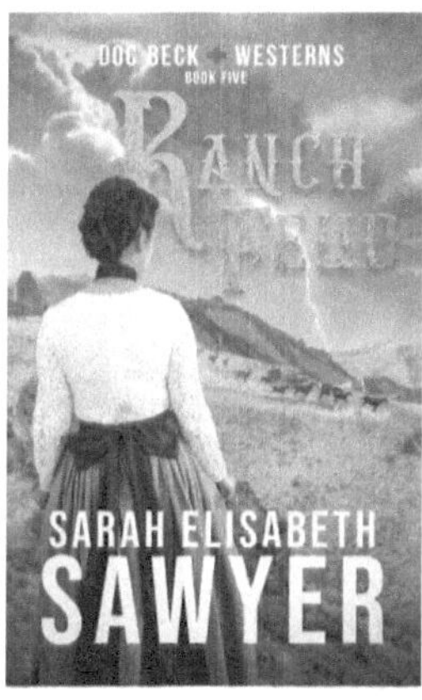

**A feud dating back to the Civil War threatens Doc Beck's future...**

Doctor Rebekah LaRoche is finally home in Wyoming—but trouble waits for her in spades, and a slim chance to return to the Omaha Indian Reservation grows slimmer when she's drawn into a feud between two powerful ranchers.

Glenn Butler and Dean Wallace hate each other's guts and have pitted their offspring against each other since birth. But it's Butler's daughter, Lilly, and her disgrace at law school that has Rebekah scrambling for answers. Rebekah wrote the letter of recommendation that helped Lilly be accepted into the college, and if she can't untangle the scandal and its connection to this powerful rivalry, she is doomed with another black mark on her professional reputation.

U.S. Senator Jeffrey Harris wants Rebekah to stay out of the young state's troubles if she hopes to have his help. But how can she stay out of something that's entangled her, threatening the last chance she has to return to her people?

**_Ranch Feud_ is available on multiple retailer sites.**

♦ ♦ ♦

*BRONC BUSTER (DOC BECK WESTERNS BOOK 6)*

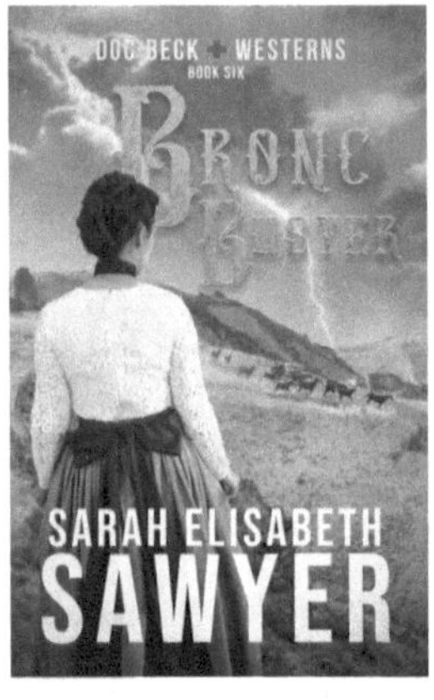


*"Sometimes trail dust is thicker than blood."*

There's nothing Just Jimmy wants more than to fit in with his new outfit on the McKinnon Ranch, and it's what Doctor Rebekah LaRoche needs, too—another piece in the puzzle of her returning to the Omaha Indian Reservation. But jealousy, a pressing contract with the U.S. Calvary, and soap soup quickly put Jimmy at odds with Steve Bowers, the new head wrangler.

Still shy of the horses they need and facing the looming contract deadline, Steve makes the bold suggestion to catch and break wild mustangs—except Jimmy and Steve aren't the only ones taking care of business in the rugged heart of the Medicine Bow Mountains.

When Jimmy stumbles upon orphaned triplets surviving off the mountain with their flock of sheep and trusty border collie, he must face not only their uncle's drunken rage and false accusation of rustling sheep —but a dark shadow from his own past.

Jimmy has a kind of wound Rebekah can't begin to heal until she understands what shaped the young man who has become her loyal companion. But are either of them prepared for a day when he will no longer be by her side?

***Bronc Buster*** is available on multiple retail sites.

◆◆◆

*THE GUNMAN (DOC BECK WESTERNS BOOK 7)*

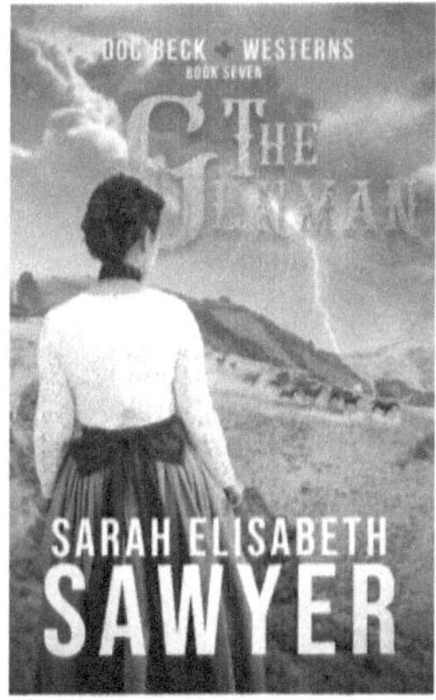


***"Whatever you do, stay out of trouble."***

The echo of Doctor McKinnon's words follow Doctor Rebekah LaRoche on her latest medical mission. But being tasked with escorting an unknown woman to an insane asylum is difficult enough; add in former gunman Cord Johnson, who claims to be the woman's brother, and Rebekah is set on a dangerous path to discover the truth about the silent woman before it's too late.

Cord Johnson's violent reputation haunts him on his quest to keep a promise made to his sister—a promise he is determined to keep after breaking so many. All he wants to do is to take Ella home to the farm their father left them and live in peace. But when a rogue U.S. marshal arrests him for murder and Doctor Rebekah LaRoche takes off with his sister, Cord must rely on the reputation of his ivory handled six-guns.

With an upcoming political meeting to state her case for returning home to the Omaha Indian Reservation, the last thing Rebekah needs is to get tangled up with a gunman and a lost woman who is unable to speak for herself. But could Cord Johnson be telling the truth? Is Rebekah set to commit the emotionally distraught woman to an asylum that will separate a family forever?

***The Gunman* is available on multiple retail sites.**

◆◆◆

*THE EXECUTIONS (CHOCTAW TRIBUNE SERIES, BOOK 1)*

"Nothing to it but a stout heart."

On a mission to bring justice to the outlaw gang that murdered his father and brother, Matthew Teller leaves the *Choctaw Tribune* newspaper for his sister to operate and plunges into an unfamiliar world of darkness and danger. Working inside the coal mines of the Choctaw Nation—one of the most dangerous places in the country—he searches for a man who may have the answers to this six-year-old mystery. But after Matthew uncovers an earth-shattering truth that rocks him to his core, he must decide what right is, and what price he is willing to pay for it.

Ruth Ann Teller knows she can handle publishing the *Choctaw Tribune*—until she loses their biggest advertiser. Now, with Matthew miles away and the future of the newspaper resting squarely on her shoulders, Ruth Ann must make a bold move to keep the newspaper afloat in her brother's absence. She sets it on a course for new success or total disaster.

Striking coal miners. Outlaw gangs. An unsolved crime. And a Choctaw family that fights for one another, and for truth.

***Shaft of Truth*** (***Choctaw Tribune*** **Series, Book 3) is available on multiple retailer sites.**

◆◆◆

*ANUMPA WARRIOR: CHOCTAW CODE TALKERS OF WORLD WAR I*

***The day I betrayed Isaac, I vowed never again to speak my native language in front of white men.***

When America enters the Great War in 1917, Bertram Robert Dunn and his Choctaw buddies from Armstrong Academy join the army to protect their homes, their families, and their country. Hoping to find redemption for a horrible lie that betrayed his best friend, B.B. heads into the trenches of France—but what he discovers is a duty only his native tongue can fulfill.

War correspondent Matthew Teller is ready to quit until an encounter with a fellow Choctaw sets him on a path to write the untold story of

American Indian doughboys. But entrenched stereotypes and prejudices tear at his burning desire to spread truth.

With the Allies building toward the greatest offensive drive of the war, the American Expeditionary Forces face a superior enemy who intercepts their messages and knows their every move. Can the solution come from a people their own government stripped of culture and language?

***Anumpa Warrior* is available on multiple retailer sites.**

*TOUCH MY TEARS: TALES FROM THE TRAIL OF TEARS*

For this collection of short stories, Choctaw authors from five U.S. states came together to present a part of their ancestors' journey, a way to honor those who walked the trail for their future. These stories not only capture a history and a culture, but the spirit, faith, and resilience of the Choctaw people.

*Tears of sadness. Tears of joy. Touch and experience them.*

**_Touch My Tears_ is available on multiple retailer sites.**

◆ ◆ ◆

*TUSHPA'S STORY (Touch My Tears Collection)*

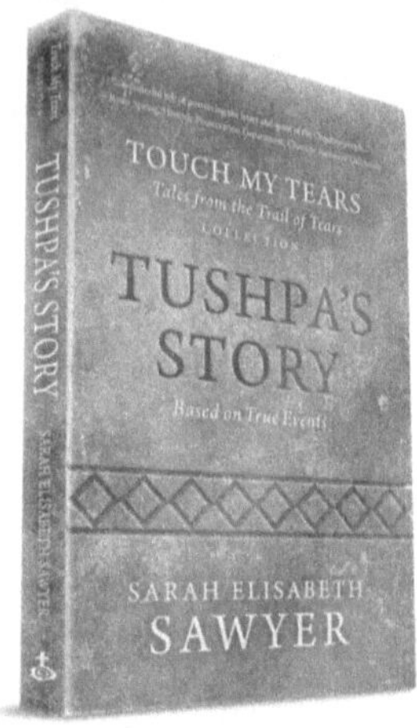

*"Protect the book as you do our seed corn. We must have both to survive."*

The Treaty of Dancing Rabbit Creek changed everything. The Choctaw Nation could no longer remain in their ancient homelands.

Young Tushpa, his family, and their small band embark on a trail of life and death. More death than life lay ahead.

On their journey to a new homeland, the faith of his father and one book guide Tushpa as he learns what it means to become a man and a leader.

But before long, betrayal from within and without rip at the unity of the band. Can Tushpa help keep his tattered people together? Or will they all be lost to sickness of the mind, body, and spirit on the four hundred mile walk?

A continuation of the anthology *Touch My Tears: Tales from the Trail of Tears*, this story follows an original manuscript written by Tushpa's son, James Culberson.

**_Tushpa's Story_ is available on multiple retailer sites.**

# ABOUT THE AUTHOR

SARAH ELISABETH SAWYER is a story archaeologist. She digs up shards of past lives, hopes, and truths, and pieces them together for readers today. The Smithsonian's National Museum of the American Indian honored her as a literary artist through their Artist Leadership Program for her work in preserving Choctaw Trail of Tears stories. A tribal member of the Choctaw Nation of Oklahoma, she writes historical fiction from her hometown in Texas, partnering with her mother, Lynda Kay Sawyer, in continued research for future works. Learn more at SarahElisabethWrites.com, Facebook.com/SarahElisabethSawyer

www.ingramcontent.com/pod-product-compliance
Lightning Source LLC
Chambersburg PA
CBHW030645190726

48286CB00008B/2659